THIS IS **NOT** A GHOST STORY

ALSO BY **ANDREA PORTES**

Anatomy of a Misfit

Liberty: The Spy Who (Kind of) Liked Me

The Fall of Butterflies

This is Not a Ghost Story

ANDREA PORTES

HARPERTEEN
An Imprint of HarperCollins Publishers

HarperTeen is an imprint of HarperCollins Publishers.

ISBN 978-0-06-242245-3

Typography by Ellice M. Lee
21 22 23 24 25   PC/LSCH   10 9 8 7 6 5 4 3 2 1
❖
First paperback edition, 2021

For all the weird girls, with the funny hearts.

For my husband, Sandy, who fights the good fight for the little guy.

And for my son, Wyatt, who has a face like a pie, with bright blue eyes filled with the universe.

Scarlett Mills Gazette, August 13, 1865

The honorable Dr. Barnaby Quince and his wife, Mary
Elizabeth, have perished in the house fire of 221 Stanton
Hope Lane on the night of August the third. The cause of
the fire is unknown, but it is believed to be due to the high
summer temperatures and low precipitation of the season,
possibly causing the combustion that sparked the deadly
blaze. Services for the doctor and his wife will be held at
the Holy Trinity Lutheran Church, Sunday, August 15,
1865, in the year of our Lord.

CHAPTER 1

Get hit by a Mack truck.

My plan for the summer. Not a goal, exactly. Because that would require a level of commitment beyond my current expertise.

It's more like a vague hope. Like that someone will invent a climate-change reverser. Or Keanu Reeves will fall in love with me. Or that Michelle Obama will one day be president. A tendril of a thought. A side note.

Still, oblivion was my goal.

You would think that in the summer before my freshman year of college I'd have no reason to be anything other than giddy. But for issues that will become clear, that was not the case for your Daffodil Turner.

Daffodil. That's me. Ironic, isn't it. Sunny, yellow Daffo-dil. As full of promise as a spring day. And yet, I am wading in dread.

I forgot to tell you! Don't assume anything. I know we are talking now, but that doesn't necessarily mean I *don't* get hit by a Mack truck. Or a city bus. Or even one of those scoot-ers everyone keeps leaving around on the sidewalk.

It also doesn't mean that what I'm about to tell you, all of it, even the supernatural parts, didn't happen.

I was like you once. Thinking there was order to the universe, structure, rules we could all count on. But this summer taught me to throw all of that out the window. You'll see. Consider yourself warned.

Maybe you think this is all a little dark? I don't blame you. But two weeks into summer, two days into summer break, it somehow feels as if I am looking at the world through the bottom of a peephole. Like those homemade cereal-box glasses we made as kids for the solar eclipse. Don't stare right into it. Look away.

But at this moment, trying to grasp a thought, like the address I am trying to remember, is like trying to claw myself one of those stuffed animals in a glass case at the Chuck E. Cheese. There. Almost there. I have it. AH! Gone! Dropped it.

Okay, the address is 221 Stanton Hope Lane. Scarlett

Mills, Pennsylvania. Yes, that is the address of my engagement. There will be no cell phone service, I was warned. I said I could just put the address in my phone. But somehow that was preposterous. I was instructed to *write it down*.

And here, standing in front of 221 Stanton Hope Lane, the weight of my commitment hits me. Maybe it's the giant gray stones at the base of the house. Or the green elm towering into the sky. Or the maple trees on the lawn looking a thousand years old.

This is a big, big place.

It hadn't looked that big, as I remember it.

Yes, I admit, it's a little crazy how this all came about. You see, I had intended on arriving at my final destination, Bryn Mawr College, before looking for work. Yes, that seemed obvious.

But somehow, when the train stopped at Scarlett Mills, the petunias and daffodils surrounding the little platform had seemed to be some kind of sign. You see, my *name* is Daffodil. So, in my mind, I suddenly felt like this was the place. Had to be the place. This was my station.

And in a rash kind of decision, the type of decision I am prone and enthusiastic to make, I jumped out of the train and onto the petunia- and daffodil-decorated platform. When I realized the college was farther up the line, I decided to make lemonade, and began my search for some kind of job. A summer job. A job that would, hopefully, pay me a handsome sum before the advent of September and my new life. The one with which I'd happily replace my old one.

Now, I know I do not get an A for planning, here. But, somehow, as these things sometimes miraculously do . . . it worked out.

Yes, going door-to-door, knocking at every address in town seemed like a positively idiotic plan. Especially with the June humidity and the bugs swarming around me and not even a one, not *one* door opening. (And, let's be honest, folks. I know some of those people were actually inside, ignoring me.)

But there was a little bit of luck, you see, just a little synchronicity that somehow led me to the farther reaches of town, even to the outskirts, and to a sweet little stone house up a long winding road. There were daffodils here, too. So you see, it was destined. And, even though it appeared little at first, as I grew closer I realized how, exactly, imposing this home was.

I could hear the sound of a conversation inside. Actually, just one side of a conversation; the man obviously being on the phone with someone who must have been extremely talkative, as he couldn't seem to get a word in edgewise.

And there was a kindness to it.

His voice.

Yes, I know it seems possibly unsafe and maybe even stupid, but I knocked. Look, I was desperate. I really did need a job, otherwise none of the rest would work.

So you see, dear friend, my dreams were fulfilled when the gentle-voiced man, who happened to be a professor, actually *did* have a summer job for me. A wonderful summer job! A job that utilized my strong suit, which is daydreaming. You see, all I would have to do is *watch the house*.

Apparently, there was some sort of renovation to be done in the back. A guesthouse was under construction. (Although, let's be honest, you could fit five entire families in the first house, but whatever.) And the price was not only right but beyond right. Right enough to pay my entire freshman year room and board, which, combined with my scholarship, would make this academic reality an actual dream come true.

I accepted immediately. It was blissful.

A moment of kismet.

Now, as I stared down that same dirt road, the house, which seemed large, yes, but normal, well-to-do-person large, seems like some kind of (pharoah's tomb) mansion. And the other houses seem farther away . . . as though the road were longer somehow.

Maybe this was a mistake. I could say I'm sick, I thought. Ate some bad tuna. Or maybe a stomach flu. I could have missed my train. Or lost the address . . .

The myriad ways I could get out of this come cascading down through my brain like those 1s and 0s in *The Matrix*. But before I can drum up the will to actually turn my body and leave, there he is on the stairs.

The professor.

He waves to me. A showy wave in the shape and size of the arc of an umbrella. "Hey, there. You made it!"

Yes, I suppose I did.

Okay, fine. Human interaction engage.

"Yeah. I'm . . . here."

"Very glad to see it!" He's a tall man with a kind of outdoorsy charm. Like he should be eating trail mix, pitching a tent, and going on a hike. A nice guy. A wholesome guy. The kind of guy who gets really excited about a new lentil soup recipe.

Oh, to have a dad such as this! Or even a dad at all. What would I have become? How would the kinks in Daffodil Turner have been ironed out? Maybe instead of feeling this particular and insistent sense of doom, I would be making cookies. Or skiing. Or translating lost texts from faraway lands. Perhaps I would be an archaeologist, dusting off antiquities somewhere between the Tigris and the Euphrates, rattling off facts about the Mesopotamian era.

I would say things like, "These fertility statues are

pre-Babylonian. Clearly Sumerian or possibly Minoan."

Instead, I am staring at the leather-elbowed professor with what can only be described as "lost puppy eyes."

"I hope the trip out wasn't too complicated. Sometimes managing these old farm roads can be kind of a Byzantine exercise," he quips.

See! Like that! I would say "Byzantine exercise."

"Oh, no, it was fine."

You can tell I'm real fast on my feet.

But he doesn't seem to mind. He gives me an encouraging smile. Reassuring. It's like he's the human embodiment of a vanilla-scented candle.

"Is this all you have?"

He looks down at my sky-blue suitcase. God, that does look old. I got it from a thrift store. It was probably hot stuff in, like, the 1960s.

Suddenly, I'm ashamed of it, seeing it through his eyes.

"Oh, yeah. That's pretty much it."

He takes a moment. "Well, good to travel light. Please, come in."

He gives me a reassuring nod and picks up my ancient, scuffed suitcase. As we're crossing the threshold, he turns to me.

"The first thing I want you to do is to set aside any of the rumors you've heard. They can be nasty." He glances out a lead glass window, and continues, almost to himself, "Nastiness seems to be the only thing that thrives in this tiny little town." And then, more jovially, "But I want to assure you . . . don't worry, because absolutely none of those terrible rumors are true."

CHAPTER

"Rumors?"

Now *this* is something I can really sink my teeth into. I am the largest fan of rumors and scandals and indignities and gossip. The only question in my mind is, what *kind* of rumors are we discussing here? Are they about the upstanding professor himself? His wife? His students? Some unseemly combination of the three? I'm going to have to pull this out of him.

"Er, I mean . . . Yes, the rumors. I've only heard a little bit about them. I can't quite say that I have the full . . ."

"Oh, dear. Well, let me just say that we have lived here now for over ten years and felt nothing, heard nothing, seen *nothing*. It's all quite sensational, really. And insulting to anyone with even the most basic working intellect."

He plunks my ancient suitcase down on the front landing. Deep mahogany wood, a staircase winding up to the second floor, oil paintings on the wall of people with fluffy white accordions around their necks and white wigs. Like George Washington's cousins. Arnold and Archibald Washington. Arby Washington. Er, Appleby Washington.

"That's why it was such a stroke of luck that you came knocking, asking for the job. A student such as yourself, matriculating at a quite exceptional institution"—he smiles warmly—"of course, none of that sensational hogwash matters to you!"

"Yes, totally sensational." I really am on a scouting mission now. "But you know how these things spread—"

"Oh, indeed." He sighs.

"Indeed! These rumors are like wildfire online. Such poppycock!"

I don't believe I've ever said "poppycock" before.

"Now unfortunately, you won't get to meet my wife, as she's already on the island."

"The island?"

"Yes, um"—he flushes ever so slightly—"it's all silly, her great grandfather, um, bought it. Probably won it in a poker game."

Yes, people win islands in poker games all the time. He seems embarrassed by his wife's fortune. My stomach churn

I wish I had the opportunity to experience such embarrassment. But I smile. He's trying to be self-deprecating.

He continues. "They say he made his money as a shipping magnate, but I have a suspicion he was more like a rumrunner. Perhaps a poppy trader."

"Well, that's—"

"Alright, so, if you don't mind, I am in a bit of a scramble to get to the train. I always seem to leave the packing for the last minute. However, we have left a few papers for you, nothing big really, just instructions about this or that. And if you have any questions, I did leave a phone number. Although, sometimes service can be a bit spotty out there."

"On *the island*. Yes, of course."

He's scurrying around now, looking befuddled and a bit unnerved. His style of dress is straight out of the academic costume department. Tweed. Classic lines. Oxford shoes.

"That's okay! Don't mind me. I'll just . . . make up my room . . ."

"Yes, yes! Take any one you choose! We aren't fussy about such things."

With that he scratches the thinning vestiges of brown hair on his head and scurries down the hallway.

"Don't forget to check the papers in the kitchen! Nothing much. Just some important tips," he assures me from what looks like a study.

A curious thing. On the bookshelf, tucked between the hundreds of books, mid-shelf, is a frog in some sort of liquid, floating in a jar. The professor notices me looking at it.

"Ah, yes. A strange gift from one of my students. A biology major. Not sure if it was a backhanded insult, honestly." He chuckles to himself.

But I stay looking at the suspended frog, his legs wading out underneath him as if in an eternal jump. Poor frog. What did he do to live out his afterlife on display in a glass jar, a musing for another, more macabre species?

A cold species, really, to keep such relics around.

"Hope you like reading! We have quite a collection of books around here, feel free to peruse anything. No use in them just sitting around collecting dust," he shouts out again, organizing, then scratching his head, organizing some more. Under his breath, I hear him talking to himself. "Let's see . . . oh yes. Right."

I stand there, not sure if I should go up the stairs or wait for him to leave to start my exploration.

I'll just wait. Seems more polite.

A cursory glance around the room tells me that someone is a meticulous duster. You could eat off the floor. Is there a maid? Does someone else live here? Or does she come maybe once a week?

CLANK!

I jump out of my skin, but down the hall the professor assures me, "Don't mind that. Just the air conditioner! I can't get the damn thing to stop making that godforsaken noise."

I have a vision of the professor staring blankly at the air-conditioning system, scratching his head while grumbling to himself. Yes, he seems like the kind of guy who would at least "give it the ol' college try."

"I'm so sorry to hurry off like this. I feel a bit guilty—"

He comes barreling in, two suitcases in hand.

"No, no. It's fine, really. I appreciate the note. And the opportunity."

He's making his exit and I really do hate long, drawn-out goodbyes, so I nod an efficient nod and assure him, "I won't let you down, sir."

He finds this amusing, nods, and gives me an exaggerated salute.

"Well, then, goodbye."

He very officially marches out the front door, leaving me there with nothing but a thud and an immediate sense of silence. A deep, overwhelming silence.

Oh my God. What did I get myself into?

CLANK!

The air-conditioning unit agrees that this is perhaps the worst idea ever.

CHAPTER 3

You may be wondering why I have chosen to fling myself into this lonely, if not pathetic, existence during the usually liberating, super fun, silly summer before college. Well, dear witness, I could tell you.

But first, let's have a look around this place, shall we? From what I can assume, I am standing next to the formal sitting room. Where no one looks to have sat for half a century, despite its impeccable cleanliness. Looming over the entire affair is an enormous oil painting of a foxhunt. Horses. Hunters in red coats. Dogs salivating. Everyone looks very enthusiastic except, I am assuming, the fox, who is hopefully hiding somewhere far outside the parameters of the painting. One can only hope he somehow escaped this particular perilous moment in time.

The walls of this room are a kind of burnt pomegranate, a textured wallpaper that blends seamlessly into the enormous, intricately carved black fireplace. There are a few oil portraits of respectable-looking relatives staring down from the centuries, looking vaguely judgmental. A striped sofa, a mismatch of wingback floral chairs, and Victorian lamps on the side tables. It really seems as if this room is waiting for a party that was supposed to have happened more than a hundred years ago.

To the other side of me, camouflaged by the wooden panels to the entry hall, is the library, filled from floor to ceiling with books, curiosities, elaborate chinoiserie vases, and plants, which I am assuming I'll have to water. The fireplace in this room is green marble surrounded by dark wood, and above it is a very calming painting of what I can only assume is the English countryside. The bookshelves are lit from within, so as to feature the curios and knickknacks. There is a globe on the table with dated place names: Leningrad, Bombay, Burma. I guess they felt there was no need for updating. Really, you get the idea. It's Earth.

This, unlike the sitting room, looks very much inhabited. Newspapers, an empty mug, a few *New Yorkers* folded to a specific article. One particularly worn-deep leather chair with an equally worn ottoman in front of it. I believe we have discovered the inner sanctum of Professor Addington. I don't blame him. It's a pleasant place. The kind of place where you could lose yourself in the brooding mercurial moods of Mr. Darcy or the endless indecisiveness of Hamlet. They would come here to you. Spend the afternoon.

Stepping back into the depths of the house, I am led through the formal dining room, which is a place for Christmas, Thanksgiving, Easter brunch, and maybe the odd dinner party. It's a deep sort of robin's-egg blue mixed with jade. A beautiful color, lit by sconces on each side of an enormous, imposing mahogany china cabinet. The deep wood dining table ends at the enormous gold-framed painting at the end of the room. Various proportions of gilded clocks are arrayed on the side table, like gold-wrapped women lounging through time, draped in gilt for eternity.

There is one funny thing here. As I lean in to marvel at the intricate gilding, there's a rush of cold air, as if someone just opened a window in winter. I stand up, looking for a vent. There's no *clank* of the air conditioner. And the feeling is gone.

It's nothing really, I know. The gold-gilded beauties from the clocks seem utterly bored by the whole affair.

It's funny in these old houses, there's no effort to integrate the kitchen with the rest of the space. The general feeling seems to have been that the kitchen was built for servants.

For "those people" who have nothing to do with the owners, other than doing everything for them. So, unlike the "open plans" you see everyone salivating over on the endless string of predictable yet somehow fascinating real-estate house-hunting TV shows, these places are closed off like a dirty secret. That's the place where the little elves make . . . *the foods!*

This kitchen, shut off from the elegant dining room by a white swinging door, is white white whitey von whitington. The floors are white octagon tile. The cupboards are white. The walls are white. The dining set in the middle of the room . . . you guessed it, white. I am tempted to open the fridge to see if the food is white. Milk. Mayonnaise. White bread.

I suppose I'll get to that later.

There's a curious little window to the side, staring out at the back porch, where there is a kind of wrought-iron dining set and a few strategically placed ferns down the stone steps to the sprawling backyard guarded by three distinct towering oak trees.

I have an odd feeling standing here looking out at that patio dinette. As if I am not the first person to stare out this little window. I can picture a dinner conversation, and me spying out over it. And for a reason I don't quite understand,

I move quickly, *VOOM*, out of the room and up the stairs.

These are the servants' stairs, I believe, leading from the back of the kitchen up to the second floor. They're cramped in a tiny space, two feet wide, and steep. A staircase made for scurrying. Constructed long before building codes. I guess they figured the servants would be skinny. No seconds for you, underlings!

The second-floor landing offers a side table. On it, perfectly placed, a chinoiserie vase, looking like it might just cost a pretty penny. The rest of the second floor is divided between two grand bedrooms, each with its own sitting room, enormous walk-in closet, and en suite marble bathroom. Between them is a grand parlor, obviously meant for visiting second-story dignitaries. I resolve to investigate all of this later, and continue up the wooden formal entry-hall staircase, leading to the third floor, which is essentially the attic. My room, or the room I decide on, is tucked into the side of the attic, a converted space with vaulted wood ceilings; a queen-size bed with a quilt; a white, peeling dresser; a painting of a cat; and not much else.

Yes, I suppose I could cheat and take one of the fancy downstairs bedrooms, but that seems like an invasion. I'm the help, after all, and the professor seems like a nice man. The kind of man who *could* be a father figure if I play my cards right. Then I would have someplace to go for Christmas. Although, let's not get ahead of ourselves. I haven't even met the wife.

I resolve to take a good look at the family photos.

I drop my belongings at the foot of the bed and sigh into the abyss. Yes, this attic is the perfect place for me this summer. This is exactly how unhappy I am. I will not have to pretend to be having a good time here. No one will be watching. No one will be expecting me to say something clever or even smile. Here, I will be able to just stare at that painting of a cat for hours, undisturbed.

Except.

At the bottom of the stairs. Two floors down. There is a giant *THUD*.

What could have made that sound? I'm the only person who's supposed to be here.

I know, I know. I probably shouldn't go investigate. But there wouldn't be a story if I didn't.

So it begins.

CHAPTER 4

As discussed, I am the only person who is supposed to be here, and I know that because that was part of the deal. I signed up for a solitary summer. A solo dirge.

Some knife-wielding murderer isn't just going to go on ahead and interrupt my entire summer of abject self-pity, right?

I mean, the audacity!

The noise downstairs sounds nothing like the clank of the air conditioner, and more like a scuffling. Yes, there was a distinct *thud* but since then, a sort of *shuffle shuffle shuffle*. Also, a muttering.

Stupid ax murderer.

Peeking over the stairwell, I see some sort of array of

printed fabrics positioning and repositioning themselves on a human figure below. Tiny painted flowers on a navy blue background, larger navy flowers on a floral background. A kind of matching mismatch of prints.

I don't think ax murderers wear florals. (I mean, possibly Norman Bates from *Psycho*?)

The human is hunched over itself as if organizing something, and its words seem to pick themselves out in twos and threes up the staircase.

"Oh well . . . now that's done . . . there it is . . . oh my head!"

There is a hat involved, a funny little orange thing with a chiffon flower, crumpled in a very purposeful way.

I should probably announce myself, say hello, or do whatever it is polite people are meant to do in this situation. But in moments of discomfort, my default mode is "overwhelming paralysis."

I stand there, at the top of the staircase, hoping the floral mystery figure somehow detects my presence. Maybe if I clear my throat . . . ? Or I could drop something? I could drop something down below. On her head. Wait. Why did I think that?

"Hellooooo?"

It's an English voice.

A Harry Potter voice.

It's exactly the right voice to go with all those patterns and that rumpled hat. It's the only kind of accent you can get away with while walking around the world as if you just fell out of a laundry basket.

"Is anyone there? Hallllloooo?"

"Um. I'm here, I guess. At least, I think I am."

The hat turns upward and beneath it there she is. A not-quite-so-elderly woman with a face the color of oatmeal and defiant red lipstick.

"Oh, indeed!" She sizes me up. "Well, whatever are you doing staring down at me like an owl atop its keep? Come down here, this minute!"

Geez. I guess she thinks she owns the place.

But the professor is the owner, right? Along with his mysterious wife?

As I descend the stairs, she sizes me up in the unsubtle way that only a woman raised with a very high opinion of herself ever would.

"My heavens. Aren't you a slip of a girl? It's as if you hardly exist!"

"That could be," I reflect.

This puzzles her and she squints at me, suspicious. "Are you, indeed, the summer help? Why, you can't even be twenty years old."

"No, I'm not."

"Well, how old are you, then?"

"I graduated high school last week."

"So, eighteen?"

"Seventeen, actually."

"Seventeen?" she tuts. "Graduated high school at seventeen . . . ? Well, aren't you a clever one?"

"Not really, I just didn't have anything else to do."

She warms to this, somehow.

"Ah!" She takes a moment to contemplate me. "I see."

As if by habit, she adjourns to the living room, taking a seat in a chinoiserie wingback chair. Blue and coral, with sparrows taking assorted positions on various branches.

"And your parents? How do they feel about this child labor?"

"There's really just my grandma, actually. She's fine with it. I think she's probably relieved."

She flattens the front of her skirt with her palms, crossing her legs at the ankles.

"And where are you from, then? Wait! Let me guess. A small but indistinct town somewhere out west but not too far out west. Illinois? Ohio? Iowa? Am I getting close?"

"I would say you're getting warmer."

She tilts her head, peering at me. "So, you're a bit sassy as well. I detect a streak of antiauthoritarianism mixed in with a singular intelligence and practiced indifference. A regular Treplev."

"Well, I'm not exactly used to being compared to male characters from Chekhov, but I'll take it."

"Ha! You do not disappoint. Alright, what state? I happen to know you can't be from further than Idaho."

"I'm from Nebraska."

"Really? I never knew anyone was actually *from* Nebraska. So it *does* exist. And people really *are* from there. Fascinating."

It's a funny thing to have someone so casually diminish everything about you. It would be insulting, I bet, to someone who took pride in where they were from. Or, for that matter, took pride in anything about themselves. Luckily, no pride here.

"Um . . ." I take to looking at my nails. "I guess I'm actually wondering who you are and why you are, um, here."

"Obviously, I'm a serial killer. Sent to add you to my collection of trophies. I concentrate on rare and exotic breeds from the middling states."

How did she know I was thinking—

She winks.

This wink might delight someone who is not me.

"It's just that I was told this would be kind of a solitary endeavor."

"And one has to wonder why a spry little girl of seventeen would want to spend her precious, singular, post-senior-year summer in such a dreary, lonesome place," she quips.

"I guess *one* would."

"She holds her cards close to her chest, does she?" I take it the "she" in this statement is me. "Well, my name's Penelope. Penelope Crisp. Penelope Persephone Crisp, if you're curious." She turns to me, suddenly. "And what about college?"

"What about it?" I ask.

"Are you, my dear, planning on attending a four-year institution wherein you might master the complexities of history, physics, or underwater basket-weaving? Or do you plan on forging a career of caretaking dreary estates for the rest of your life?"

Suddenly she remembers something and begins rummaging through her bag, gliding into the pantry. I follow her, confused. But as she is speaking, she keeps reaching in and out of her bag, piling up mason jars on the shelves.

She notices my questioning gaze and in response simply says, "Oh, jam, you see. I always have extra so I just give it to the professor. You will absolutely love it. Apricot preserves. Strawberry, of course. Blueberry. And even a kumquat one; I thought I'd try my hand."

I quit counting jars at eight, but she certainly doesn't stop retrieving them. I guess if there's a zombie apocalypse, I can just survive on jam.

"And college? What are your plans?" she repeats.

I sidle into the hallway, not really wanting to tell her my entire life story, or even a fourth of it.

"Well? Have we given up already? No college?"

She really doesn't mince words, does she?

"I'm expected to attend college in the fall," I acquiesce.

"And which one, might I ask?"

"Bryn Mawr."

At this she lights up like a birthday cake. "OOHHHH! Bryn Mawr! Well, why didn't you say so?! You buried the lede, you silly girl!"

I have no idea what those words mean but am grateful she's finally not looking quite so sternly down that long nose of hers. I was beginning to feel like I was on the witness stand. But now, now I am a member of some form of club. I guess I will not tarnish this newfound warmth by divulging my plan to run in front of a moving vehicle sometime between now and Thanksgiving break.

"Well, now that I've delivered the delicious and, might I say, exquisite jam, I must be going. I really just wanted to pop by and see that the new girl had arrived." She quickly walks back through the hallway and begins collecting her things. "Bryn Mawr! What a funny little thing! You know my cousin went there and quickly became a lesbian! Absolutely stormed into it! Are you planning on becoming a lesbian?"

"I wouldn't put it past me." I shrug.

"Oh, you kids! You're all so maddeningly open about everything. It makes me long for the days when we were ashamed! Ashamed of our own shadows!"

And now she's put on her expensive orange crumpled hat. "Well, I'm just down the road. Don't hesitate to drop by if you get bored contemplating your future identity or whatever it is you plan on doing here on your own. My door is always open. Ta-ta!"

With that final gesture, she's out the entryway and down the front stairs without even a look back.

She gets to the end of the gravel driveway before I decide. I like her.

CHAPTER 5

I've never been very good at sleeping. Even in kindergarten. There were always too many things to be excited about. Or scared of. For instance, being left. What if you put your head down and went off to happy dreamy cloud land . . . woke up and, poof, everybody was gone? Just like that?

And what about tonight? I'm just supposed to lie here and easily fall asleep in my little converted attic?

Yes, I understand there are two perfectly wonderful and grand bedrooms downstairs. We've been through this. Not only is there nothing museum-like or breakable here, this attic fits my state of being.

But it isn't easy to sleep. This is more of a toss and turn situation. I can't seem to get comfortable and there is that *one* thought, that very specific one, that I have been avoiding all day.

Here, on my first night, that thought wants to drag itself out of my brain's recesses and into the open. But there is no way I am letting that happen.

Nope. No, sir.

The problem is, it's quiet as a tomb here. Silent enough to allow just about any thought to pop into your head. Like, if you went deep enough, you could solve the mysteries of quantum physics. You could invent a replacement for money. You could do just about anything.

But most especially, you could think that *one* thought. Until it killed you.

Maybe if I just get on my feet, walk around the room, stretch my legs. Or maybe even head outside.

Yes, what if I go for a little stroll. A moonlight stroll. Why not? This is a tiny little town, out in the middle of nowhere, far away from the hurly-burly of city life. It's *totally* safe. I could just take a moonlit constitutional.

Have I ever taken a nighttime stroll before in my life? No, no, I have not. Does it seem imperative I do right this very moment? Yes, yes, it does.

Before I know it, the outside is pulling me like a magnet. *Come to me, come, and I will soothe you. Come to me, and there will be peace.* It's tugging me down the stairs and through the entry hall, out the front door. *No need to get dressed, there's no one out there. No need to lock the door, this is country life.*

I saunter out around the house, to the back, where the grass grows across the vast expanse of lawn into a field of some kind of reeds, **restless**, waist high, blowing this way and that—a single organism, a sea of reeds.

It's beautiful, really. This choreographed dance to the wind. This midnight show.

This must be what has drawn me out here in my pajamas. Out here, in the moonlight expanse, just a slight breeze. A summer breeze. The night air cooling the day.

But that's when I see it.

"See" is the wrong word. Feel. That's when I feel it. Whatever *it* is.

How to describe it. It's like a sudden rush of feeling. A *slam*. And suddenly I am aware of being watched. And I know exactly where I'm being watched from.

I'm being watched from inside the house.

The completely empty house.

CHAPTER

Before we go any further, let's get the facts straight. The underlying reality of the situation. The underlying reality of *me*. Because otherwise none of this is going to make sense.

Some people, like the professor and his absentee wife, for instance, come from a long line of money that's presumably been there since the *Mayflower* and accumulated nicely over the centuries. And some people, their dads maybe invented Post-its, or fidget spinners, or what have you, and now they live in a giant mansion with a man cave and a pool in the back with a Ping-Pong table in the pool house.

I am not those people.

I, dearest reader, am from that class of people that has to track every dime, every cent, every new pack of underwear, every extravagant Frappuccino, every bank balance, every parking ticket. Payment in and out, every bill, etc. etc. etc. And, so, what that means is . . . let's say someone like me gets into a really good college out on the East Coast somewhere. A college with people named Muffy or Binky or Blair. Unlike dear Muffy or Binky or Blair, I would have to figure out, to the letter, exactly how such a feat could be accomplished.

In this case, the feat being the tuition, room, and board. I would have to somehow patch together a quilt of scholarships, grants, and employment to succeed at such an attendance. Our friends Muffy, Binky, or Blair, you see, have *advantages*. I have no such thing. So I would have to cobble this whole thing together myself. Out of nothing. Out of magic. Out of dirt.

Look, I'm not asking you to feel sorry for me. I just hope you will see this for what it is. Which is threading the needle. A unicycle act on a tightrope. Underneath, no cushion. No kind words. No second chances.

And this, here, this employment. This summer caretaking job in a lonely house on a winding street outside mainline Pennsylvania, this is the opening act. The one upon which all other acts rest. And it happens to be a huge amount of money. To be here. That's the lucky part. I got lucky when I knocked on this particular door. It's more money than I had ever even dreamed of acquiring on my own, straight out of high school, summer before my freshman year. In fact, it's almost a suspiciously high amount of money, for the task at hand, come to think of it.

But I need it.

Desperately.

So, *mes amis*, that is the context through which I would like you to view the forthcoming events.

Simply put, I'm in a tight spot.

Let's say, for instance, I somehow magically decide *not* to throw myself in front of a vehicle during my first semester. In such a case, my only escape from the horrible past is Bryn Mawr. It is my ejection hatch. A new start. So, there can only be two possibilities: (1) shuffling off this mortal coil; (2) starting a new life in college. Suffice to say, I haven't quite decided. I am keeping my options open. But there is one thing that is absolutely, positively not an option. And that is . . . going back to Nebraska.

But this job, here, at this strange place is an essential piece of the puzzle. I cannot quit. I cannot flake. I cannot leave.

Which is why I am trying extremely hard to explain to myself right now that what I am feeling, coming from over there, inside the house, is not actually real.

CHAPTER 7

If this were a real thing I was feeling, and not, as is logical, a figment of my imagination, it would be described first, even though I can't actually *see* it, as a live thing. Some sort of entity. A being.

Whatever it is, this nonexistent thing, it is staring daggers at me from inside the house. It is saying to me in a voice that cannot be heard but only felt: *Get out.*

All five senses are engaged in an instant.

The information that I'm getting from it doesn't allow me to think of it as anything *nice*.

It is dark. And it is focused. Fixed, somehow, on me.

It is coming from inside the house. I know this even though I can't see anything you would describe as eyes, mouth, or a face. It is trained on me. It is there, focused. Impossible to see. Impossible not to feel.

I am not welcome. Somehow I know that. In a sixth sense we must have unlearned as a human species. It doesn't want me here. It is angry with me, or maybe anyone, being here. In this place. On its territory. All of that, those facts, in a great sudden sweep across the yard from the house. How do I know that—in an instant—in a way you never could know, really?

It's impossible. But there they are. Clear as a bell.

Whatever that being is in there, it wants me out.

What will happen when I go back in?

Because I *will* go back in.

I, quite literally, can't afford *not* to go back in.

I want to close my eyes. I want to close my eyes and open them again and have whatever that *thing* is be gone. But I can't. Because I'm suddenly filled with a cold fear that causes goose bumps to rise in a wave over my body—a fear that when I close my eyes and then open them again, that *thing* will be closer. Right upon me, just next to me.

A deep shiver racks my body.

Yes, I know, all of this cannot be happening.

Is this a hundred years we are standing here? A month? A week? A day? Or is it just a second, a momentary flash? Is time stopped in this endless moment?

Is this a standoff?

A confrontation on a kind of pause?

I tell myself, firmly this time, that if I close my eyes, if I just close them, I will then open them again and it will be gone. Because the thing is not real. It will not be closer. It will not be right next to me. It will not be in me. (This last thought comes from some unexpected place and makes my stomach roll.)

This is a kind of prayer I'm saying to myself, so loud in my head but not out loud. *Please be gone please be gone please be gone.* . . .

And I close my eyes.

Then snap them open.

CHAPTER

Have you ever been in a car accident? Do you know that feeling, that feeling of time slowing down even though time has not slowed down but you could just swear it had, it had to, because every moment seemed like a minute?

That is the time it takes for me to close my eyes and open them again.

A century.

Decades. Whole lifetimes come and go in the time it takes me to shut my eyes and then open them again.

And when I open my eyes again it is . . .

gone.

No feeling. No presence. No malevolence. No form.

As if it had never been.

As if maybe I were dreaming.

And isn't that, honestly, the most possible thing?

I glance down at my watch. 3:23 a.m.

Let's just think about Occam's razor for a second here. Is it *more* likely that a noncorporeal malevolent spirit fixated on me from inside the house? Or that in my current wretched state I *thought* I felt something there that clearly wasn't?

Occam's razor says the latter.

What happened was something from my imagination.

A daydream.

A thing that could never actually exist.

This is what you would tell yourself if you had a job that you couldn't leave and had to be here, in this place, by yourself, for the rest of the summer.

This is what you would have to tell yourself.

And if you were reeeeeeeally good at fooling yourself . . . say, if you were the kind of person who could spend her life not thinking about certain things . . . it would work.

So, this is when you would sigh, put that moment in a box, shut it tight, tell yourself none of it really happened, turn, and walk back inside.

Quickly, up the stairs, to your attic bedroom, under the sheets—and back to sleep without a care in the world.

And it would almost work.

CHAPTER 9

This morning I have an important meeting. I have to come across as entirely professional. No fidgeting. No awkward silences. I am a professional girl in full control of her faculties who is here to organize things. A pragmatic girl. A logical girl.

After all, this is what I'm here for. This is the job. Or part of it anyway. The note in the kitchen explains the timeline of construction, the first set of meetings, and a basic outline of the project. It occurs to me that they've really entrusted me with quite a lot. They have confidence in me! (I'm not sure why.)

Nevertheless, I am here to organize the entire thing.

The grand renovation.

Yes, the kindly professor and his wife had in mind that whoever would stay here, in this exquisite place, would also oversee the extensive renovation of said place. This is what they are paying the big bucks for.

Oh, you thought they just wanted me to exist here in this clearly not haunted place? No, no. I am here to work. Or to oversee the work. Which is also work.

Now, I don't know about you, but I am awkward with guys. Not any guys. Not older guys, like the professor. And not guys my age or younger than me. They are fine. No problem there. No. I am awkward with guys who fall between the ages of, say, twenty-five to fifty. Guys in baseball caps. Guys who watch sports. Guys who high-five each other.

It's not that I don't like them, exactly. Or that I feel superior to them in some way. It's that they make me nervous. Like they are just about to snicker behind my back and tell a lewd joke about my body. Like they are secretly all part of some bro club where whenever a girl walks out of the room, they all look at each other and share a laugh of some kind at her expense. Yes, I know I sound paranoid. Or weird. And that, statistically, this would be impossible for *all guys* between twenty-five to fifty to be that way.

But I am not some bastion of great humanity like Mother Teresa or Desmond Tutu over here. I am just a person with my own foibles and idiosyncrasies and this happens to be one of them: a discomfort with all men between the ages of twenty-five and fifty who might watch sports.

So sue me.

The funny thing about this highly compensated job here (and this is something you would think I would have considered beforehand) is that this kind of man is the *only* kind of man I will be dealing with.

I should have thought of this. To not think about this was ridiculous. Or absentminded.

Or, perhaps, purposefully painful. Masochistic. As if I am punishing myself for a behavior I know, fundamentally, is wrong.

It's impossible to really know what I was thinking.

In fact, now that I think about it, it seems odd to me that I would just randomly get off the train when I did. But somehow it was like I was simply compelled, compelled and then propelled. Like a decision made and not made. A fugue state. A sleepwalk.

A dream.

It's like this: There are some people who really *think things through*. They analyze an idea, weigh it, turn it over in their hands, wiggling it back and forth like a prism, peering at every facet, every multitude of possibility. I am not one of those people.

Now, some would call me rash. I would say that I am a

participant in life. I make a strange decision and act on said strange decision. Of course, it is not always the best decision.

Like now, for instance.

All of this is dawning on me as I am woken up by the sound of someone pounding on the front door, rather forcefully, before I open the door and am met with what appears to be the head bro, or the "guy in charge," and four of his bro compatriots. All in jeans. Two in baseball caps. One in a ripped, sleeveless T-shirt. The "guy in charge" has strawberry blond hair, short, and looks like he could coach Little League. Totally Mr. Normal. Basic model. Straight off the conveyor belt.

I think, if I were to see myself, I would see a girl with her mouth twisted over to one side in a kind of pained expression of ineptitude. I would see a semicircle of bros around her at the front door, looking extremely impatient and annoyed, shifting their weight from one side to the other. And I would see the "guy in charge" sizing me up and deciding, fairly quickly, that I obviously must not be the one in charge but the assistant to the assistant of whoever actually was in charge.

"Um. Hello . . . miss. We're from the MoniCED Company Builders. We're s'posed to start work today. Out back." He gestures.

Yes, I know what "out back" means.

"Of course! Yeah, they're . . . I mean *we're* expecting you."
Now he's just looking at me.

"Mike. Nice to meet you." He puts out his hand in what is meant to be a gesture that is returned. Oh! I know! I'm supposed to shake his hand! That's what men do. They firmly shake hands. They solidify it. Whatever it is. Maybe everything.

I grab his hand and shake it. But now I am shaking it too long. He is looking at me. I put my *other* hand over our hands. Like I really mean it. Like he's really super welcome. Like I've never before seen another human.

Yup. Miss Awkward van Awkwardington. At your service.

He nods for an uncomfortable eternity and then takes his hand back.

Phew. I didn't know how I was going to get out of that.

The four guys behind him continue their pantomime of looking up, shifting their weight, and looking anywhere but at me, finding interest in the flagstones of the front walkway. The moss between cobblestones. An ant on the front stairs.

"We can just go around if you want."

"Go around?" I ask.

"Yes. Go around. The house. We can go around the house. To start work in the back."

"Yes, yes, of course! Go around. I understand. That would be great. Please do. Be my guest. Go on . . . around."

He nods, looks back at his guys. A subtle look. They start to move en masse toward the side of the house, the mossy pavers leading through to the back.

I stand there, not offering anything. I think I am supposed to offer something? Or maybe I'm not. I'm the boss! Why should I offer anything? No. They're on their own. Is that how you do it? You see, I've never actually *overseen* anything. I've been in more of an avoid-being-overseen position for most of my life. School. Grades. Teachers. Papers. Extracurricular activities. Debate. Chorus.

But this. This is all uncharted territory. A world of mystery where people shake hands. A job!

Mike, aka the leader of the pack, gives a little wave and heads around the house. None of them say anything, but clearly that is not going to happen until I am out of earshot and then they all laugh and make fun of me. I know how this works.

On the street, down the driveway, the orange and white truck with the insignia on the side "MoniCED Company Builders." Not the catchiest of names. That's for sure. Sounds almost . . . medical.

It occurs to me a normal person would be happy right now, considering the nonevent that definitely didn't take

45

place last night. A normal person would feel safer. Ah, yes. They are here. The men are here.

But that is not the feeling washing over me. Nope. The feeling seems to be more of a widening of the circle. Like . . . there's the nonexistent entity staring out at me from inside the house and now, *in addition* to that, there is a group of men staring at me from the outside.

I think of a soft bunny rabbit, which is prey to the fox and the hawk.

CHAPTER 10

The first day of the renovation is uneventful, other than me trying to pretend that I am unaware of the guys working on the guesthouse. Most of the time I just spend going from room to room, trying to act casual. Now I am reading a book. Now I am "washing the dishes." (There aren't any dishes.) Now I am contemplating the universe in this wingback chair. I'm trying to look like a respectable person. Not a freak.

When the guys finally leave, I feel an overwhelming sense of relief. Why? I have no idea. They weren't paying attention to me in any way. Not once. There really was no reason for me to enact this charade of being a person all day.

I wonder if this is specific to me, or if everyone feels this way at a certain point. Are we all just sitting around pretending to be normal? Pretending not to go through a thousand different emotions in the span of half an hour? I really can't be the only one feeling this way. I mean, I doubt I can be. I hope I can't be.

I have a very serious night planned involving the wearing of sweatpants and watching *Ancient Aliens*. It is impossible to ponder any earthly issues when clearly we are all descended from the Anunnaki tribe. *Don't you see? All of a sudden we were given democracy and harvesting from some extraterrestrial force from above. Otherwise, how could Homo sapiens possibly have been the one form of the human species to survive? We weren't even the biggest! Our brains weren't even the biggest!*

These are the things I lovingly contemplate in my daydreams.

Also, maybe I can convince myself that whatever it was I definitely did *not* feel last night was, perhaps, just some sort of alien life-form. A being from somewhere near Orion's Belt. Perhaps a star traveler from the Gemini constellation. Nothing to worry about. Just studying. Taking notes to bring back to the mothership.

All of this is going swimmingly until the sound of wild-eyed conspiracy theorists on Netflix is interrupted by a subtle noise coming from somewhere near the back of the house, behind the pantry.

A scratching noise.

I hit mute, cutting off a very fascinating theory about the first man called "Adamo" by the Sumerians, created by the Anunnaki as a slave race to mine for gold. I am in the middle of reminding myself to rewind this particular part of the show when I hear it again. Subtle. *Scritch scritch scritch.*

Not like the sound you would imagine from, I don't know, some sort of monster outside the house trying to get in and eat you. Just a little scratch. Perhaps, maybe, a cat. A sweet little cat just trying to make itself known. Maybe hoping for a saucer of milk.

These are the fluffy warm rainbow thoughts I force myself to think as I follow the sound out through the hallway, through the kitchen, and to the pantry. The pantry is just a little tiny white room off the kitchen, stocked with cans on the shelves, a broom, a mop, and a few cases of bottled water. Why there would be a cat in the pantry is beyond my grasp and, of course, there is no cat in the pantry.

But the sound of "the cat" is definitely coming from the pantry. It's not getting louder, exactly, so much as I'm getting closer to it. And as I'm getting closer I'm beginning to realize the sound is not coming from *inside* the pantry so much as it's coming from outside the house, seemingly trying to *get* inside the pantry. So you see, "the cat" must be outside.

That is perfectly logical.

It is at this moment, my dear friends, when I have to make another decision. Here are the choices:

Number one: Go outside and see what, exactly, the sound is.

Number two: Go back in the living room and continue to watch *Ancient Aliens*. Turn the sound up and pretend I do not hear anything.

Hmm. This is a difficult one. While I don't really want to go outside into the dark night with a heretofore unidentified scratching sound . . . I also don't think I'll be able to actually relax.

Because the funny thing about the scratching sound is that it does seem to be getting louder. More insistent. And, there's another thing. I notice that the closer I get to the scratching sound . . . the louder and more insistent it gets. Like "the cat," which is obviously not anything more terrifying than a fluffy little feline, seems to know I am on the other side of the wall, getting closer. And . . . the closer I get, the more "the cat" seems to want to come in.

I decide to conduct an experiment. I close the pantry door, walk a few steps into the kitchen, and listen for the scratching. Dimmer. Softer. Slower. Now . . . I walk a few steps closer to the pantry, open the door, and move in toward the scratching sound. . . . Louder. Faster. More frantic.

So.

Somehow this thing, aka "the cat," on the other side of the wall is aware of me. Aware of my presence. And animated by my presence.

It is here that I make an executive decision:

Go to bed.

If I go upstairs to bed, then I won't hear the scratching sound and if I don't hear the scratching sound, then it, quite simply, doesn't exist. I can always watch *Ancient Aliens* on my laptop with my headphones on and not a care in the world. Also, if the scratching sound gets worse when I get closer, then it falls to reason that the farther away I get from the sound, the more likely it is to stop.

I am in the middle of telling myself this when the scratching sound abruptly stops. As if whatever the scratching sound was, it read my thoughts and decided to agree with me. Now the house is completely silent.

Okaaaay.

I find myself backing up out of the kitchen, out through the hallway, up the stairs, up the second-floor stairs, and to my humble little bedroom attic abode. I find myself desperately grateful for technology and the lull of my sweet laptop. Before I allow myself to feel anything approximating fear, I snap my headphones into place and get back to the lore of the ancient Sumerians.

But I do have a quick thought.

In the morning, I will check outside, on the other side of the pantry, and then I will see there is nothing there.

Of course, that is only logical.

CHAPTER *11*

There's a dangerous time in the morning when I wake up, in that moment between dreaming and waking. It's a time I've noticed I can easily think about the thing to never think about back home. You see, my conscious mind is really quite good at squashing down any unwanted thought and burying it under the rug. But my unconscious mind, my dreaming mind, well, that's where the trouble is.

I came all the way out to the middle of nowhere to not have to think about this thing and, by God, I am going to stick to it.

Maybe if I set an alarm it will wake me up so quickly, so abruptly, that my subconscious mind will be scattered away. Hurried off in a fit of the living. I'll banish it.

I know. You'd like to know what it is. I understand. But I know what you'd think if you knew about it. I know what you'd think because it's exactly what I'd think. I'm not immune to it. Believe me, this is better left under the rug.

Just keep it there.

But maybe I can give you the first part. The part I just dreamed about. Maybe the first part is something nice. Something you could believe in. Something you could love.

That part starts, would you believe it, at a carnival. A state fair. The Nebraska State Fair to be exact. Every fall in Lincoln, Nebraska, all the pig owners and pumpkin growers and children's art classes and roller coasters and Zipper rides and sailing ships rides come into town, set themselves squarely on the meadows outside of town, and wait for the fun to explode.

And, growing up in Nebraska, that is just what you'd do. You would, as a child, look forward to it, ask your folks about it, when is it coming, when is it coming? Then, as a teenager, you would discuss it with your friends. When are we going? Are we all going as a group? The first Friday? Or maybe Saturday? Are we meeting before?

On this particular night, fall of ninth grade, we were all going as a group. Five girls, from Pound Junior High, in it together. Yes, I realize Pound Junior High is an unfortunate name. Believe me, we've heard it. Dog Pound. Roof Roof! Bark bark, how is the doggy pound? It's okay, we're over it.

The important thing about all of us girls having gone to Pound is that there was another junior high school on our side of town, Irving Junior High, that fed into our soon-to-be high school. Lincoln Southeast High School. Now, Irving Junior High was the rich kid's junior high. The kids there lived on Sheridan Boulevard and all grew up in what I can only imagine were enormous bedrooms and additional playrooms piled up to the ceiling with toys and video games and a thousand stuffed animals.

It was inevitable that we would hear bits and pieces from Irving, but just enough to keep our curiosity piqued. Now, Pound Junior High had a few upper-middle-class kids but I was not one of them. I grew up with my grandma in a ranch house near the eastern edge of town. Yes, I had a few toys. But there were hardly piles of them. And we went to church a lot. A. LOT. Sometimes my grandma would actually speak at the church, like do that day's readings from the Bible. So, you know, it was all pretty serious.

We can talk later about why I lived with her. Then you can judge.

At this moment I'm letting you hear about, we're at the Nebraska State Fair. The sun has gone down and the lights of the Zipper are flying up and down behind my friends, who are all crouched together, whispering excitedly. I dip my head in.

"What? What are you guys talking about?" I whisper.

"They're there," my bossy friend Callie replies.

"Who's there? Where?"

"Right there! Don't look!" Callie gestures with her head, subtle, and I follow to what looks to be a group of shadows, at the foot of the Zipper.

"Did they see us?" Callie whispers, serious.

"I don't think so. Who is that, anyway?" I ask.

"Who is that?! Who *is* that?" Callie looks at me in astonishment. "That is only *the* only people from Irving Junior High we care about. And that we have to get to like us. Next year. Or we can kiss high school goodbye."

"Really? Why? Why would we kiss high school goodbye . . . ?"

"There he is. Did he see me?" Callie is practically hyperventilating. But our mutual friend, Sally, placates her.

"No, you're fine. He didn't see you," she soothes.

"Who didn't see you?" I ask.

Callie rolls her eyes at me. "Zander Haaf."

I meet this declaration with a stone-cold look of . . . nothing.

"Zander Haaf! You mean to tell me you've never heard of

Zander Haaf?" She rolls her eyes at me again. Callie rolls her eyes a lot. It's how she got to be the queen of Pound Junior High.

Sally leans in. "It's okay, I hadn't heard of him till last year, either."

"That's because you never pay attention." Callie is somehow getting meaner by the minute. "Is he looking at me now?"

Sally and I look over to the teenage figures entering the Zipper.

"No. They are definitely not paying attention," I admit.

"They're just getting on the ride," Sally adds.

"Fine." Callie huffs off in the direction of the funnel cakes.

Something about Callie huffing off gets the attention of one of the Zipper guys from Irving. He looks at her. Then looks to where she came from. Then looks at us.

Then looks at . . .

me.

And I know, right then and there, without a description, without a word, without a thought . . . that *that* is Zander Haaf.

And Zander Haaf is still looking at me.

CHAPTER *12*

Before I get out of bed this morning in this clearly not haunted house, I would like to take a moment to picture Zander Haaf. In that moment. The moment in front of the Zipper.

He's not tall, exactly. But he's not short. Medium. And his hair is medium, too. Medium brown. Not dark brown. Not blond. Just medium brown. Like the color of a walnut. There's a kind of flip to his hair, too, longer in the front. But nothing crazy. And he's not even wearing anything special. Jeans. An olive green jacket that has lots of pockets for hiking or some other dreamy thing.

So, you see, nothing much.

Except.

Zander Haaf has sea-green eyes. Not olive green. Not gray green. Actual sea green. So, basically, his eyes are like a window into the vast depths of the ocean and the mystery of the world.

It's the eyes. All of it.

You don't believe me that I can see those Ocean Eyes from all the way across to the Zipper but I do. And so does Sally, and the rest of our friends. Sally exhales, a whisper.

"Oh my God. He's looking at you. Daffodil. Oh my God, he's still looking at you."

And I, because I have no self-esteem and am feeling wildly self-conscious, look away. But I want to look back—I want to look back—I want to look back. . . .

"Okay, he's still looking. Now the ticket guy is hurrying him. Okay, relax, now he's gone," Sally reports.

Somehow I feel like I have the wind knocked out of me.

Sally looks at me. "Daffodil. He was, like, totally checking you out. Like a stalker. Do you know what this means?!"

Sally is looking at me now like I'm Taylor Swift.

Callie comes back from the funnel cakes, empty-handed.

"No funnel cake?"

"Nope. If I'm going to make Zander Haaf fall in love with me I can never eat again," Callie declares.

Sally glances over at me. We share a look. The international expression for *never say anything about that ever again.*

But in that moment, standing there at the Nebraska State Fair sans funnel cake, looking up at the Zipper lights going around and around at dizzying speed, I feel something I haven't felt before. A kind of anticipation. A kind of fear. Like the inside of my skin has just been replaced by a jungle full of butterflies. They fly past each other and up and down and it could be that I am on the Zipper, too, flying across the sky at lightning speed.

And I wonder what will happen next year, sophomore year, and if I will ever see Zander Haaf again. And, if I do, if he'll remember me.

The girl from across the fairgrounds.

CHAPTER *13*

I could wait until the construction team gets here before I go outside and determine if there is anything of interest on the other side of the pantry. I could wait to discover if "the cat" left any scratches and, once it's clear there is nothing there, I could go back to assuming that the whole episode was purely in my overly vivid imagination.

But I am curious.

Also, I don't really want to get dressed before going out there and, if I go now, I can just pj it up. The sun is bright gold over the yard out back and before I know it I am stepping over the blades of grass, getting drops of dew all over my flip-flops. It's not that easy to tell where the outside of the pantry would actually fall, but I'm trying to triangulate a little from the kitchen windows, to the living room windows, to just in between.

Ah, yes, here it is! The pantry doesn't have windows so it must be here. Right here, clearly the other side of the pantry, facing out toward the field.

It really doesn't look like there's anything there so I turn around and happily, gladly, trot back to the kitchen steps. See? It was all just a funny little figment of my imagination. Probably too much *Ancient Aliens* burrowing its way into my subconscious. Mystery solved. All logic restored.

I am just about to ascend the stairs when I notice a little thing, out of the corner of my eye. Just a tiny thing, not really anything to write home about.

There, not on the outside wall of the house but underneath it, underneath the place where I was looking for scratches, is something uneven. Something bumpy in the dirt and the morning dew grass.

And now, as I get closer, I begin to make it out.

You see, there are little bits of crabgrass all over the side of the house, a pale green, some of it almost seeming gold in the morning light with the dew reflecting the sunlight. This blanket of crabgrass surrounds the house and wades off into the field where there are taller reeds and weeds and a few stray dandelions. But it's a consistent covering, almost like a light green rug, around the outside of the house.

Except underneath the outside of the pantry—over just a bit from where I'd been looking. That seems to be the exception. And it's not that the crabgrass had just stopped growing at that very spot. No . . .

It's more that it's been ripped out.

It's more that the crabgrass that was there before was suddenly disturbed in a most cruel and unusual manner, leaving chunks of dirt and grass and roots to the side and all over the ground nearby.

And, if you look closer, it starts to appear that the reason why such damage was done to the sweet little crabgrass is that something was . . . clawing at it.

Something substantial.

Something much, much bigger than a cat.

It looks, almost, if you step away and look at it with an objective eye, as if some thing was, dare I say it, actually trying to dig its way down *under* the wall.

Under the wall and into the house.

And, whatever it was, it seems like it was pretty desperate, pretty adamant, about getting in. On a kind of mission.

I stand there piecing this together and trying not to let it turn into a thought that will catapult me running toward the hills.

"Morning."

The sound makes me jump three feet into the air.

"Oh, sorry, didn't mean to startle you." It's Mike. Leader of the pack. Head honcho. Construction maestro. Captain of the team.

"Oh, yeah. I . . . um. I'm fine."

He looks at me, sizing me up. "You okay?"

"Yeah, I'm just. I thought I . . ."

I just let this trail off. I feel like if I ask him about the crabgrass or tell him about the scratching noises he'll just think I'm an idiot. Some paranoid girl with a wild imagination and no friends. A shut-in.

"Okay if we start work? I know it's a little early, but you *are* up. . . ."

"What? Oh, yeah. Of course. Yes. That's what I'm here for. Please do. Start work. I'm just. I was just on my way to the store."

He looks at my pajamas.

Suddenly I realize my pajamas are kind of revealing. Like, my whole leg is right there, and the other one too. Both legs. Just out and about. Is he looking at my legs? (Of course, they're not shaved. I'm not Beyoncé.)

And I'm not wearing a bra. Or underwear. (I'm not the queen of England, either.)

"After I change! I was going to change and then, after that, head down the road and grab a few things at the store. . . . Need anything?"

He smiles, shaking his head a bit. Maybe he just thinks I'm nervous. Or hairy.

"No, I'm fine, thanks for asking." He adds, "I can give you a ride if you want. It's over a mile. That walk."

"Oh, I know. I just. Sometimes it's nice to go for a walk. Morning light."

He doesn't know what I mean. Of course he doesn't. He never went to my shrink. My shrink never told him, "Hey, it's a good idea to get out in the morning to counter depression. Morning light. You must try to get some morning light." Yes, she told me it's imperative to get morning light and yes, I maybe do it once a month. Nobody's perfect.

"Okay, then. We'll just get started." He nods, assuring.

He walks back around the house to where I'm sure the other guys are waiting for him, shuffling around.

I take one last look at the destroyed crabgrass under the wall. It could be anything. A possum. A raccoon. A dog even. It could be anything. I'll google it. This is silly.

It's just a natural thing. An animal. An animal from nature.

Nothing sinister at all.

On my way into town I decide the loneliness is getting to me. That must be it. Just because I decided to come out here all on my own doesn't mean I have to actually be alone the whole time. I could invite someone over! Some other humans who would come stay with me and help sway me to the obvious conclusion that everything is normal.

But who?

I specifically left "back home" to get away from everyone. And the thing I'm not thinking about. If I invite anyone from back home, then that is out the window. But what about this? A family member. A cousin. Two cousins even. A cousin is the kind of person you can randomly email and get to come to some house in the middle of nowhere, right? Because family.

It just so happens that I have two cousins who might actually do such a thing and are not too annoying. They live with my aunt and uncle in Chicago and they have never been mean to me for being from the middle of nowhere. In fact, they've always been pretty nice about it. Intrigued. Curious. Ready with questions about what the kids at my school wear and what we say and how the social structure is ordered.

They go to kind of a fancy school because my uncle, aka the one I'm not related to, is sort of persnickety about that stuff. Like, he's the kind of guy who takes pride in his kids going to a really good school and having "authentic experiences" when traveling or whatever. Which makes me think . . . If you want your kids to have such "authentic experiences," why don't you just send them to an "authentic" school rather than a billion dollar one? But perhaps his authentic-meter can only be filled out of the country. Either way. They're nice. And, right now, they might have to come here and save my life and/or sanity. I make a note to myself. Yes, I will reach out to them.

Her name is Abby and his name is Ollie. She's one year older and definitely seems like she might be president one day. Ollie is my age and is more like the kind of kid who wears Converse high-tops and plays the drums. Really well, mind you. I'm not kidding. You should see him. I saw a video my aunt posted and it was kind of like everyone at the school talent show was silenced into submission by his otherworldly ability on the drums.

But there are no drums here. Just "a cat" or something outside, some mysterious scratching noises and a bunch of super-bros working on the guesthouse. I make up my mind to call my cousins. It will be half a plea and half a description of a glamorous getaway-slash-sleepover with no parents. Maybe I will bill it as an "authentic experience."

In town, there's a little café called "Mabel's Muffins," complete with a mural on the wall of a forest made entirely of pastries. I have to wonder if this was Mabel's idea or if somebody just randomly came into town and asked her if he could paint a muffin forest on her wall. You never really know. Maybe she built the café just because she was looking for a place to showcase her pastry landscape.

As I walk in, I'm pretty sure that the aforementioned Mabel is standing in the corner over the coffeemaker, in an apron that says, "Kiss Me, I'm Desperate." But she doesn't really look desperate. She looks nice, actually. An ash-blond bun in her hair with wisps everywhere. She looks like someone you would cast in a movie as the hardworking hero's wife. She works hard, too, to keep bread on the table, but she never loses faith and she's loyal as a lion. Before the hero goes off to fight zombies, she'd look at him reassuringly. She would know that he would never make it through the zombie apocalypse, but that "a man's got to do what a man's got to do" and she'd let him go. In the end, she'd be the only one to survive. Here, in the muffin forest.

But then, something changes in the air and, for no apparent reason, I become overwhelmed with anxiety.

I'm anxious at the idea of talking to her. Anxious at the idea of talking to anyone.

What if she starts asking questions about why I am here and what I am doing and why I am all alone?

No, no, I can't.

I can't talk to her.

The room seems smaller, shrinking somehow, and suddenly I am terrified of any interaction whatsoever.

I won't be able to explain myself.

She'll judge me.

She'll know.

As if by a kind of catapult, I shoot myself out, in one fell swoop, out of the café and into the street. I don't look behind me, for fear she might say something to bring me back.

No, I can't talk now.

I can't do any of that yet.

I look down at the sidewalk as the few townsfolk walking around come by. No, don't talk to me. Don't make eye contact. Leave me alone.

It's a strange sort of thing to describe, this sudden fear. It started to happen after—

It started to happen after the thing that cannot be said.

There is no understanding of it and no history of it.

There is only one certainty to it.

It's crippling.

I had the idea that I would go into the little used bookstore in town, but now that seems impossible. A ludicrous idea! Then I will be begging for a conversation.

No.

No, not that.

Best to just turn around and go straight back home.

There, I'll be safe.

CHAPTER 15

Halfway back to the house, the memory keeps trying to claw its way out of its little box in my head. But I won't let it. And this time I have a strategy. I'll take out just the part I like, like a scientist examining a specimen. A good part. I'll start with that. Then I'll put it back down on the shelf before the bad part. A selective memory. A spotlight shone on just one teeny-tiny instance.

And this is the part I choose:

It's sophomore year at Lincoln Southeast High. The two middle schools, Irving and Pound, have coalesced into one school, this high school. Everyone is still trying to find their footing. How do I fit in here? Who am I? Am I a loser? Am I one of the cool kids? Are *they* the cool kids? Wait, if they are the cool kids, what does that make me?

You get the picture.

I was in a precarious position. Even though I had come from a slightly normal, not horrible echelon at Pound Junior High . . . Irving was considered the cooler school. By default, they would be the cooler kids. And we unfortunate Pound kids? Well, we could only hope. Maybe, just maybe one of the Irving kids would "choose" us. Maybe they would lift us up out of the depths of mediocrity. Maybe . . . but it was a long shot.

Already, one of my two friends, the meanest one, Callie, had ditched me to become part of the in crowd. The summer between freshman and sophomore year, Callie got a job at a community pool as a lifeguard. Guess who the other lifeguards were. That's right. Irving kids. Apparently bonding occurred. And Callie left our friendship behind. Not a word or an acknowledgment. Just gone. Like the wind.

Let's face it, we all knew she would drop anyone like a hot potato on her way up the rungs of the popularity ladder.

Now, my other friend, Sally Milhauer, she would have stayed my friend, and she and I could have held together in a kind of middling, not total loser situation.

But over the summer *she* switched schools.

I know!

Her mother decided to send her to a Catholic school,

which was insane because Sally was half Jewish. I think she was trying to get back at Sally's dad, who had moved to Omaha and married his SoulCycle instructor.

So, just because Sally's dad couldn't resist that lady jiggling around shouting affirmations in spandex, I was faced with the proposition of spending my time in high school alone. A total outcast, possibly the biggest loser in the universe.

But this was all changed, praise Jesus, when a funny thing happened to my biology requirement. You see, I didn't realize I couldn't take biology and computer science in the same semester. Why not? I mean one day obviously they will be one and the same. In the future, when we are all cyborgs. However, Lincoln Southeast High had other ideas for my education and they booted me out of the one, throwing off my entire class schedule and landing me straight into Mr. Eckdahl's 10 a.m. biology class.

Now, this was the second day of school, so the lines in that class had already been drawn, the seats taken, alliances made. And yet, there I was forced to stand, in the doorway, with my paperwork explaining to Mr. Eckdahl that I had to not only interrupt his class but actually take his class.

As Mr. Eckdahl scratched his head, looking out over the sea of two-person tables, I saw a funny thing out of the corner of my eye . . . one student, in the back of the class, frantically gesturing to his tablemate. Swatting him away. Forcing him to move!

Then, as befuddled Mr. Eckdahl turned back to the classroom, he seemed to see an opening he hadn't seen before: a seat free, there in the back. He gestured to me to take this very seat.

I took the seat, the seat that had just been frantically vacated, and couldn't even bring myself to look up to see who the mystery person who had made sure that that seat was empty actually was. But as Mr. Eckdahl began his lecture about cell division, I managed to peek out from behind my newly acquired textbook to see who the guilty party was. And there he was. In the flesh:

Zander Haaf.

Yes, *the* Zander Haaf. The one who my antifriend, Callie, had been freaking out about at the state fair one year ago. Zander Haaf. Aka, the guy who every girl in all four Lincoln high schools was obsessed with, in love with, and engaged to marry in their imaginations.

And he emptied that seat next to him . . . just for me.

CHAPTER 16

I am just about to get into the second phase of that particularly vivid memory when the house begins to show itself through the trees. The construction guys are hard at work in the back, the sounds of hammers and some kind of power tool breaking into my heartwarming memory. Their hard hats roam this way and that like yellow ladybugs.

It occurs to me that I haven't really bonded with "the guys" at this point. They probably don't realize I have terrible social anxiety. I wonder if I should explain this to them. But it seems a bit much. I mean, it assumes they care, which they probably don't. Also, there's something strange about them, something kind of on autopilot.

In any case, I'm happy to have them there, making all that racket. Normally, of course, I would be up in arms about the constant noise but, really, it's better than the perpetual silence that settles over the place at night. It's also a lot better than that mysterious scratching I was telling you about. You know, the scratching that I *obviously imagined.*

I notice something on my way up the path, passing by the white construction truck of the contractor, Baseball Hat Mike. In the back of this truck, there in the back seat, is a duffel bag full of baseball equipment. But the gloves are a bit small. Like, kids' size. Ah! He *does* coach Little League.

Of course he does.

I notice the name on one of the uniforms. It says the "Southside Sea Cucumbers." I am sorry but I have to find out which of these Little Leaguers came up with that name so I can give them a trophy.

I wish my curiosity had led me only to that quaint and comforting fact. But, alas, the world is a cold and unfeeling place. My gaze goes from the sweet Sea Cucumbers uniform to something else, something much more sinister.

An ax.

Yes, of course it's perfectly natural Baseball Hat Mike would have an ax. He's a contractor. I mean, what if he has to fell a tree in the line of duty? It could happen, right?

But there is something about it. Something that stops me in my tracks. Like the ax has meaning. Like there is something I should know about that ax. Or something I should remember. The cool steel of its blade seems to wink at me.

"Everything okay over here?"

I look up and there he is, Baseball Hat Mike. I guess he's probably wondering why I am peering into his truck and having a strange mental dissonance over its contents.

"What? Oh, yeah. Of course. Sorry. I was just, uh, zoning out, basically." This is my default. Just act like a space cadet. That seems to be an acceptable pigeonhole for me for someone like Mike. Nothing threatening. *Just a girl.*

"Oh, yeah. Okay." He nods and I take the opportunity to walk backward toward the house, tripping on a tree stump.

"Whoops. Yeah, I didn't see that. Obviously. Because it was behind me."

Baseball Hat Mike just stands there.

"Hey, can I ask you a question?" There's nothing mean in his voice. It's almost like he feels sorry for me.

"Uh, sure."

"Why are you here all alone?"

It's a direct question. I will say that. But it's not something I can really answer in full. Without possibly having a midday breakdown. In front of the guys. Who probably wouldn't even notice.

"Oh, I'm just. Well, I start college next fall. Summer job."

"Ah." He sort of squints. "You didn't want to go to Europe or stay with your friends or something?"

Now, this seems prying. Like, how does he even know I have any friends?

"Um . . . well, this kind of helps me . . . be able to . . . actually go to college."

And that is true. Without this job, no room and board. Without room and board, no college. Pretty simple.

"Ah. And where are you going?"

"Um. Bryn Mawr."

He whistles. Just a whistle. No comment.

"Wait. Why did you just whistle?"

He smiles and shakes his head. "Sorry. It's just an expensive school. I guess I wasn't thinking. I didn't mean to be rude."

I just noticed something about him, something I didn't notice before. He's not a bad-looking guy. I mean, some girls, not me of course, would even find him attractive. In a freckle-faced kind of way. Again, and I feel this is important, not my type. But . . . I can see how he might be someone's type.

"How is the . . . work . . . coming along?" Do you call it

"the work" in a situation like this?

"Oh, it's fine. It's gonna be nice, actually. They'll like it, I think. He will. I don't know about her. I only met her once."

I'm assuming he's talking about the professor. Funny, no one ever seems to have anything nice, or anything really at all, to say about the wife. I wonder why that is? Is it unconscious misogyny or is she really, like, not a nice person? Aloof? Full of herself? Snooty?

"What are you guys doing now?" I am trying to seem like I care. A normal person would definitely care.

"Oh, we're digging a hole. For the foundation." He contemplates for a second. "Hey, did you see a dog out here or anything?"

"Excuse me?" That came from left field.

"I dunno. There were all these claw marks around some of our equipment."

The blood stops in my veins.

"Kind of big ones."

Wait. Big ones? Like big claw marks?

"I know. It sounds weird. It's just . . ." He trails off.

"Uh. I don't have a dog. I didn't see a dog."

We both just stand there in silence for a second. Neither of us wanting to seem too weird talking about mysterious claw marks.

"Yeah, I dunno." He shakes it off. "Well, better get back to work." He starts off toward the back, leaving me nodding and smiling.

Nodding and smiling like someone who isn't thinking about kind of big claw marks.

Inside, the house is just as I left it. I shake my head. Why am I being so dramatic? So there are a few claw marks on the side of the house. This is the country. There are animals. And animals have claws. Not such a big deal, really, is it?

And the other night, the "presence" I felt . . . can't that just be chalked up to some new-environment jitters and the general spookiness of a dark night? I'm really just a kid afraid of the dark. That's all it is.

I pick up the landline because, yes, the professor is so old-school he actually has a landline. I dial my cousins, Abby and Ollie, to fulfill my diabolical plan of forcing them to come visit me. It's strange, though, when I call them. There's a *beep boop beep*. "We're sorry, the number you're trying to reach is not in service." Well, that's weird. Probably I just got the number mixed up. I vow to try again later, on my cell. I can never remember anyone's numbers, anyway.

I take solace in going through the cupboards. A snack to hearten me while I watch my latest conspiracy obsession online. Although I can't seem to find what I'm looking for. I could have sworn there were some salt and vinegar potato chips that had my name on them in here. I rustle through three different bottom shelves before sighing in defeat and reaching for a chair. I don't know why they make shelves so high. It's as if girls don't even exist! Dragging the chair across the floor, I hear the men outside yelling to each other. Something about a missing hammer. As much as I'm not used to hearing full-volume yelling from man voices, there is a comfort to it. In this quiet place. Maybe this is where I discover an appreciation for the male species. Or at least, less of a fear.

The top shelf is as cluttered as the rest and I am just about to give up on those tantalizing chips when I notice something tucked in the back of the shelf.

Odd.

It's a little glass jar. Inside is some kind of . . . organic material.

I reach in and grab the glass jar, teetering a bit on the chair.

It's a mason jar, with a burlap kind of string wrapped around it. Inside are what looks like dried flowers, some kind of charcoal, and a little note, a kind of scrawl. The scrawl isn't a language, or even an alphabet, I recognize. It's almost like some kind of ancient rune writing . . . something you imagine would be found at Stonehenge. I peer at it, wondering if this was left by the professor. Is it his? Or his wife's? I never met her. Maybe she's batty? Eccentric.

Mad.

All of this comes over me at the exact same moment the organic material crystallizes in my head. Oh yes. I know what this is. I recognize that scent. Copper. Oh, I know it well.

It's blood.

Not much of it, just about a teaspoon. Here, at the bottom of the glass. Almost black. And in it . . . a few odd hairs. As if plucked. Meticulously placed. In the blood.

Well, this certainly is not my salt and vinegar chips.

I know some people might get queasy at the sight of blood but, trust me, I've had enough periods to just see it as a regular old nothing. Oh, yes, blood . . . that happens once every twenty-eight days and is really annoying. Associated with cramps, crying, a desperate need for chocolate, and the throwing out of at least one pair of underwear a month. The grossness of blood is not a thing for me. It's more like the inconvenience of blood. The *ugh* of blood.

But, that said, you have to admit, whatever this is . . . this little glass jar of runes, blood, hair, and burlap. It is a bit strange. I mean, this has to be some experiment. Akin to the frog, ever swimming in his jar in the library?

It's a spell, some dark part of my brain whispers. And I scoff at the thought.

But perhaps this wife *is* into witchery. Maybe there are books strewn across the house with magic potions and spells. Witches aren't inherently evil, after all. It's just the patriarchy that made us think of them that way.

A potion. That's really all it is. A nothing thing.

But just as I am about to think the next comforting thought, the cupboard door swings open and the jar falls to the floor.

The kitchen door frames Mike as he looks up at me, there on the chair, having just dropped the glass jar, now shattered on the floor.

"Sorry . . . I just wanted to ask you if you've seen a hammer around. We seem to have misplaced one." He looks around. "Did I scare you? I'm so sorry."

"No, no, it's just . . . um, a hammer?" I try to act normal. "You know, I haven't seen one. I haven't been looking. But . . . if I see one, I'll be sure to leave it out for you. Maybe by the shed?"

"Yeah, okay," he replies. "Again, I'm really sorry. Here, I can help you clean it up."

"No!" If he comes closer, he'll see what it is. "No, it's fine. I've got it. I'm just . . . clumsy, I guess."

I shrug. This is what I do. I make myself small. I sigh. I swat it all away.

Just a girl.

Just an absentminded girl.

Why do I feel the need? Why does the presence of this jock-like guy make me feel the need to erase myself? Or make myself slight?

I look down at the glass shards below.

The blood and hair just sort of congealed and lay as a clump there on the white tile. The tile spreading out in little octagons across the floor.

A thought crosses my mind.

Was this a spell? Was this jar some sort of voodoo offering?

And then:

If this was a spell . . .

Is it now broken?

CHAPTER 18

After cleaning up the random, slightly disgusting shards of glass jar of organic material and scribbles, I decide to take a shower, relax, and google. Whatever that thing was, that lunacy in a jar, I can probably find it on the internet.

I spend an inordinate amount of time going down about five different rabbit holes from ancient rune paintings to spell-casting sites that will actually cast a spell for you. For one hundred dollars. One thirty if it's a double-cast spell. Which means they cast it twice in one day. Very powerful.

Insert eye roll emoji here.

By dusk, I still haven't found the exact same combination of items in that glass jar or what they might mean. The closest I have found is a spell called "return my love to me."

While it does involve hair, blood, and a glass jar . . . there is no charcoal or rune markings involved. This may take a little more doing than I expected.

Or giving up. That is, also, a possibility.

Hmm. Give up or try?

The ancient question.

Pros of giving up: don't have to do anything.

Cons of giving up: won't know what that thing is.

Also, pro of giving up: won't be giving that thing more energy . . . possibly might forget it.

Also, con of giving up: maybe it matters! By ignoring it, I will never know.

Okay. So far I am leaning heavily toward giving up.

There is, also, the small matter of my latest conspiracy binge: *Flat Earth: The Great Lie*. I cannot tell you how happy I am to sit around and watch a bunch of yokels going on about falling off the edge of the world. I mean, call me simple, but it's the little joys that count.

I resolve to give up.

Down in the yard, the guys have all gone home for the night. So . . . no more pesky interruptions about missing hardware or tools or whatever you call it.

Somewhere in the middle of a screed about conspiracy by a balding man in a beige Members Only jacket, I fly away into dreamland. Up, up, and away.

Tonight I get to dream about things that happened before the bad thing.

On this night, I dream about the first few weeks of biology class with Zander Haaf.

You see, at first, I pretended not to notice Zander. I pretended that I couldn't care less. That I had no idea he was *the* be-all and end-all of every girl this side of the Mississippi. Oh, I was cruel! I was better than cruel, I was indifferent. And, somehow, the more indifferent I was . . . the more bent out of shape Zander Haaf became.

It got so I was just used to acting like that—calm and apathetic—and he was just used to acting his way—interested and slightly agitated. He would write me notes. I would barely look at them. Sometimes, if I'd finished my work and there was no lecture, I'd scrawl something back. Some tiny thing. But just enough.

And Zander would be filled with hope.

It was strange. Because I was never the best-looking girl in the school, not even close. Like, I could rattle off a list of girls, Tiffany, Juliette, Charity, etc., etc., who were *way* more good-looking than me. And it's not, at all, like I was even the most popular. In fact, I was always considered a bit weird. Strange. Eccentric, my grandmother would call it. But she was just trying to make me feel better. Let's face it.

So, to have Zander Haaf, king of crushes, slayer of hearts,

writing me note after note after note in biology, which I had the audacity to ignore . . . made no sense. It was like the world had turned upside down and, all of a sudden, people who never even knew I existed were saying hi to me in the hallways between classes. People whose names I'd only heard. People who played sports. People who belonged to the country club.

And, you know this about me by now, I did not belong to the country club. I belonged more to the country barnacle. My house was what a real estate ad would call "cozy," by which I mean "crappy." The paint was faded from white to gray, and the house always seemed a little bit like it might just fall over on itself.

So, happy day! To have, for once in my life, some kind of fantasy life where the high school royalty deigned to actually see me . . . all because of Zander Haaf. Well, I don't have to tell you. It was like being lifted off an anthill onto the tippy-top of the rainbow. And I loved it. I lapped it up. I never thought I'd have to slide down that rainbow again. Happy days were here to stay!

You see. These are the things I dream about. These are the days I have trained myself to play on repeat over and over to just a certain point. If I can keep them to that certain point. Then it is glorious. It is a glorious defense.

But make no mistake.

It's a defense nonetheless.

And this shiny, happy defense is whisked away in what seems like a wind, or a draft, or a shudder, and I find myself awake in my humble attic bed once again.

Although, now the window is flung open and the night air is rushing in. Yes, that must be what woke me. Just weather. You see, totally natural.

I sigh and move toward the window but, when my feet hit the ground, I notice the floor looks different now. Worn, weathered. I look around the room.

Wait.

The paint on the wall is faded, peeling. I move to turn on the light, but there is no light switch. Instead, there is a hollow rectangle where the light switch is supposed to be.

This is a dream, yes? This must be a dream.

And in my dream, I tell myself not to panic. It's okay. This is just a dream. Let's play along. Okay, I'll get my phone. I'll turn on the flashlight mode.

Now, looking around the room with the light, it's as if the house is abandoned. Even the painting on the wall is not there, just a pale rectangle where the painting used to be.

I'll play along with this dream, because it's just a dream. I'll inspect the rest of the house.

And, indeed, the landing is empty, decrepit. Down the now wobbly stairs, one stair even missing. And the downstairs bedrooms . . . the grand bedrooms . . . empty. Completely empty. Not a bed. Not a chair. Not even a curtain.

Ah, yes, this dream. I will go along with this dream. Now I will go along, down to the first floor.

Here it is. The downstairs study. Desolate. Not a desk. Not a book. Nothing.

And the front door. Ajar.

Clanking back and forth in its frame.

And the spiderwebs.

In this dream, which must be a dream, the spiderwebs cover the dusty chandelier in the dining room, the rafters above the entry. Vast, intricate spiderwebs. As if the spiders have taken over for centuries. A spiderweb haven. An altar for Arachne.

The creaking of the front door in its frame leads me out, drawing me out the front door and down the outside stairs. It's not even cold tonight, a summer night, the moon in a crest, the constellation Scorpio in the distance; you can tell it by the arc near the horizon, it's one of the easier ones to see in summer.

Yes, I am still game for this dream. Yes, I will look back at the house in this dream.

And so, with the slip of a moon and Scorpio behind me, I turn to see the house.

A decrepit house. A house falling in on itself. A house abandoned.

If this weren't a dream, well, this would be a moment to have a heart attack. A gasp. A choking off of air.

But, you see, just put it in a dream. Put it in a dream and you can walk slowly back up the stairs, inside the house. Put it in a dream and you may walk steadily through the cobwebs, up the stairs, up the second set of stairs, up into the forlorn old attic and close the dusty window. Put it in a dream and shut off the phone and lay back in the bed and understand that none of this is happening.

And everything is perfectly fine.

CHAPTER 19

"Yoo-hoo! Is someone there?! Oh dear, have I come too early?"

My not so heavenly slumber crumbles as the distinctly English voice echoes off the wooden walls.

My mind wants to attach itself back to the dream last night, the forlorn, desolate, decrepit dream . . . but British voice won't allow it.

"Hallo? Yoo-hoo!"

Ah, yes. My friend. The eccentric lady from down the road.

What was it?

Penelope. Yes.

Penelope Persephone Crisp.

A bit early to come poking about, but perhaps nine a.m. is late for her. My grandmother used to wake up at five in the morning. Sometimes even four-thirty! It was positively grotesque!

"Hello, hello? Anybody home?" Her chipper voice hoists itself up the stairs as I peek over the banister.

"Yeah. Yes! I'm here." I do sound a bit rude. I feel like I have to be more polite because she's English. "I'll just be a moment."

I'm sure I look like I just fell out of a laundry basket.

"Hi there." I come down.

She looks at me.

"Still asleep, are we?" she admonishes.

"Yeah. That's right. Guilty." I repony my ponytail.

"I must say, those jingly contrivances on the doors make such a fuss. I thought they would surely wake you," she comments.

"I'm sorry . . ." I squint at her. "Jingly things?"

"Yes, you know. Those exotic tokens all over the doors."

"Exotic . . . tokens. . . . On which doors?"

I open the front door and take a look.

"Hmm. That's odd. I hadn't noticed those before." I look at the silver jangling things attached to the top of the door. "You'd think I would've noticed them."

"Indeed," she adds. "You know there's one on every door."

I continue inspecting them. At the bottom of each one there's a blue circle, like a kind of target. Or an eye.

"There is?" I look at her.

"Oh, yes. I'm sure the professor brought them back from one of his many voyages. He's quite the world traveler, you know. And his wife. Although, at least she doesn't brag about sleeping on the ground in the dirt with grubs everywhere. The professor tends to romanticize these sort of things, you know. . . ." She trails off.

I notice she's wearing the exact same thing she was wearing the other day. Hmm. Maybe as you get older it just doesn't matter. Or maybe you just forget. I know I'd wear the same thing every day if I could get away with it. Or maybe she has multiple identical things. Like Steve Jobs. So she doesn't have to think about it.

"Well, do you know what they are? I mean . . . are they like . . . dream catchers or something?"

"Dream catchers! Oh, heavens no. I don't think so. Seems a bit touchy-feely for these academic types, don't you think?" She peers at me.

"Yeah, I guess. I suppose I can google it." I smile.

"Oh . . . quite."

I get the distinct impression she has no idea what I'm talking about. I have the idea to offer her a cup of tea. Isn't that what English people do? Cup of tea? Have some tea?

Put the kettle on? If movies teach us anything, it's that the English run on tea.

"Maybe a cup of tea?" I ask.

"Oh, good heavens, no! I'm on my way." She grabs her orange hat from the side table. "I was just popping by on my way into town, thought I'd make sure you were getting on."

"Um. Yeah. I'm getting on." In fact, I was getting on so well I was asleep, lady. But I don't say that. "Doing fine."

She holds a moment, contemplates. "To be true, dear, the professor did tell me to keep an eye on you. Not in any sort of suspicious way, mind you. No, dear, not at all."

I'm barely putting this together in my muddled morning head, but she continues.

"He's just such a kind man, truly. He was a bit worried you might be lonely. So, you see, you shan't be rid of me, try as you might." She smiles, a wink in it.

"Oh." I think about it. "Sure. Yes, that's . . . fine. Nothing like a little company, I guess. No, please do feel free or whatever."

She sizes me up. There is something about her that comes across as wise . . . as if you could say anything you'd like and she'd see through it. She just knows. She's been around. She's seen it all. Truths. Half-truths. White lies.

"Oh, good. Well, I'm pleased to hear it." She gives me

a pursed smile and a nod, and then makes her way to the front door.

"Bye, then. Nice to see you," I say, again trying to be polite.

"Yes, dear. Always a pleasure."

She disappears out the door and the silvery, exotic tokens jangle. It's strange I didn't notice them. In a way, it makes no sense.

I go to the back door. Yes, there's one on that door, too. Yes, it also jangles.

But how could I have not noticed before? Was I so caught up in my infinite musings? The jangling is not subtle. Not in the least.

I certainly didn't notice them last night in my empty-house dream. But why would I? It was just a dream, Daffodil.

Both my lips are doing that thing where they scrunch up on the side . . . in dubious thought.

It's only when I open my laptop and proceed to google that I have my answer.

It's a talisman.

From either Turkey or Greece.

They're meant to be hung on the outside of the house as a protection from evil spirits.

Well, I can certainly see the professor or his wife picking

97

them up in the Grand Bazaar in Istanbul. A memento of the journey. A trinket. Nothing more.

And then, despite the fantastical nature of the idea, antithetical to any academic worth their salt . . . I can certainly see them placing the talismans on the doors. Just simply in the spirit of the thing. Not for any specific reason. An exotic token. A conversation piece. A gas!

The professor is not the superstitious type. I'm sure his wife just placed them around for fun, or for possible dinner conversation. After all, just because you place tokens from a souvenir shop, or the Grand Bazaar, all over your house, doesn't mean you actually believe in whichever spell or symbol they're meant to represent. It's just a thing that rich people do. Collect things. Collect items and showcase them.

Nothing more.

CHAPTER 20

The worker guys are back, pounding away in the backyard. I notice that the boss, Mike, the Little League coach, hasn't arrived yet. I guess that's one of the perks of being the boss. I resolve to try to be the boss, no matter what I decide to do. Maybe I will just be the boss of watching conspiracy videos.

Right now, for instance, it seems I am the head honcho of lying in bed. No, no, it's not really normal to lie in bed for approximately two days. That's clearly not a healthy thing for a seventeen-year-old person to do. But something seems to have happened to me where my back stays glued to the top of the bed and can only wheedle its way over to gather a few pillows and open up a laptop and start exploring the world inside said laptop, rather than the world outside my bed.

That world is scary. That world has uncertainty and voodoo charms and construction bros and the thing that cannot be mentioned. But this world here, this world behind this blue light, is safe and endless. This world takes me back to ancient aliens, through the fall of the Roman Empire, through medieval times with possible dragons, through a dozen wars between England and France, the discovery of the New World, up until the present. The time when the blue screen was invented to teleport me out of reality. And there is some reading, dear friend, I have taken the time to read a book a week . . . lest you think I'm just eating bonbons all day. But that, too, involves lying in bed. So it's positive, yes. But not exactly contributing to my cardio.

I did make the effort, once again, to try to reach my cousins on the phone. Abby and Ollie. This time from my cell. If I could just get them down here, maybe they would love it and we would have a blast! It would be like a Norman Rockwell painting. Abby and I would gossip and giggle all day and I'd let Ollie play *Roblux* until his face turned blue.

But, again, that same *beep boop beep.* "We're sorry, the number you're trying to reach is not in service. Please check the number and try again." And I checked. And I tried. Checked. Tried. Checked. Tried. But nothing. The number I have is officially wrong and I am officially annoyed and officially sick of hearing that dumb automated message.

Fun fact: Three nights ago, in the middle of the night, I thought I heard that scratching sound again. But this time I was not fooled into getting out of bed. No, no, sorry. No, you cannot coax me out of my sweet warm cocoon with just some scratching.

You see, I have learned. The explanation is that there is a rather large dog, or possibly even a cat, who has some obsession with something in the ground there. That is the simplest explanation. Occam's razor. And, since that is the simplest explanation, that is the most possible one and the one I have trained myself to believe.

Problem solved.

And, now, having had the experience of the desolate empty-house dream, I know that it's probably wise just to stay in bed at night. No reason to go anywhere. Just sit tight. Snuggled beneath the sheets.

Yes, it is possible I could explore other options. Of course, but let's not get carried away when the entire canon of both novels and cinema is at my disposal. And that new subscription to CuriosityStream, which means entire series on the Silk Road, the rise and fall of the Roman Empire, and the Wars of the Roses. Not to mention podcasts.

For instance, right now I'm enthralled by the true story podcast of a southern California suburb where a rich, sweet interior designer has been seduced by a homeless man posing as a doctor. You see, you can't make this stuff up. So, yes, there may be scratches, but my armor is my apathy. And my addiction to the internet.

Just as I am about to start my day by listening to episode three of said podcast, there's a knock at the back door. Hmm. That must be one of the construction guys. Well, my job is to oversee this baby, so that means I will have to not only get up out of this blissful bed, but actually get dressed, comb my hair, and make sure I have not slobbered all over myself somewhere in the night.

The pounding continues as I descend the stairs, and there, framed in the little window of the farm-style back door of the kitchen, is Mike. He squints at my figure coming toward him.

"Late night?" He smiles.

"Um, yeah. I was up . . . studying," I defend myself.

"Studying? Really? Over the summer?" he asks, crinkling his forehead.

Wow. I guess Mike is a bit of a nosey noodle.

"Um, actually, I have a project I'm working on. It has to do with the mesh of civilizations in southern Spain, Andalusia, and how, perhaps, the Alhambra declaration is what directly led to the fall of the Spanish Empire."

He looks at me for a moment.

"I'm researching it for a possible history dissertation. It's never too early to start thinking about it. I'm planning on doing a dual major in history and religion." That part is at least true.

"Guess you're ahead of the game. Don't most people take the summer before college off?" He now looks honestly concerned about my well-being.

"Most people probably have more money than I do." This comes out before I can stop myself. Stupid. What a vulgar thing to say! My grandma says you're never supposed to talk about money.

"Wait. Are you getting paid to stay here?" He looks up at the house, as if the house could answer.

"Um, yeah. And to just make sure all . . . this . . . goes okay, I guess." I gesture to the construction.

"This? You mean us? Are you here to watch us?"

"Oh, no, it's not—"

"Make sure we don't steal the soaps?" He's irked now, or maybe he's joking.

I try to laugh it off, not wanting to get into a scuffle.

"Don't worry, sweetie. No one's gonna steal the soaps, or the figurines, or whatever other tchotchkes are floating around."

Sweetie?

He continues, but all I can hear in my head is that word. "Sweetie." Clanking around all over the place.

". . . My guys are honest guys. And I am, too." He looks at me, suddenly serious.

"Yeah, I never . . . um, thought anything like that, actually . . ."

"If anything, you're the one who needs looking after."

This takes me by surprise.

Also, *sweetie*?

"Yeah, you." He nods. "Little girl like you, all alone in this place."

"Oh, it's fine I'm—"

"Hell, I'm worried about you." Again, he squares off, facing me. I realize he's a bit of a space invader. Like, he's not observing the stay-three-feet-away rule. He's definitely a little too close for comfort.

"Oh, well. I'm adjusting, it's—"

"Is there an alarm system or anything in here?" He looks around the doorway. Again, space invading.

"Um, I don't think so. The professor . . . never said anything about it. I'm sure he would've." I hadn't thought about it. Honestly, this guy is officially freaking me out.

"Okay, this is what I'm gonna do. Every morning, when I come, I'm gonna check in. Make sure you're alright. And at the end of the shift, before I leave, I'm gonna make sure you're squared away, safe and sound. *And* . . . I'm gonna give you my number. In case there's any trouble. Especially on weekends." He nods, a dad nod, assuring.

"Um. Okay." I guess he's just trying to be nice?

Maybe he's just a really nice guy.

But still . . . "sweetie."

"Alright then. You take care." He turns to join his crew, but then turns back. "Hey, you seen that hammer?"

"Excuse me?"

"That hammer. Still can't find it," he answers.

"Um, I don't think so. I did look," I assure him.

"Hmm. Weird." He walks away, taking his baseball hat off and scratching his head. It's a red Phillies hat. Of course.

I want to say something to him, a final witty note. But all I can think of to say is, "Do you like baseball?" which I think we can all admit is a pretty obvious thing to infer judging by his coaching kit as well as his baseball hat.

So, instead, I'll just stand here looking natural in my sweatpants and wonder if he noticed the coffee stain on my T-shirt. From yesterday. No need to wash it, it's just me here, right? Mostly.

I don't know if I should be vaguely insulted or flattered by his sudden interest in my well-being. Or by "sweetie." Whatever I'm supposed to be, it seems like I'm a little bit of both. That's the thing about emotions, they're never just one of this and one of that. Never pure mad. Or pure happy. It's always a little bit of both. There should be more words to describe these things. Like bittersweet. Or sadjealous. Or gratefulinsulted. Maybe my problem is that there never seems to be the right word for what I'm feeling.

Or the right words just haven't been invented yet.

I reach out to close the back door and shut this whole interaction down when I notice something real quick. Something I remember distinctly noticing was there just last night.

The eye charm thingy is missing.

The one from Turkey.

I look at the foot of the doorway, down the porch steps to the dirt, and out at the yard. But no. No jingling blue silver anything. Nothing.

Nowhere to be found.

I look out at Mike, having a conversation with his crew.

No, he wouldn't take it.

I mean, didn't he just say he wouldn't take any "tchotchkes"?

Of course he wouldn't.

And maybe I look around at all the other outside doors to find the Istanbul eye thingies and maybe all of them are gone, too. All gone. Not a one left.

And maybe that could freak a girl out but, then, that girl might not be me. Because I am just going to assume that perhaps some of the crew thought they were kind of nifty and decided to take a few of them home to their wives and/

or girlfriends. Or maybe someone passing on the road there took a shine to them. Whatever the case may be, it's not a big deal that they were there and then not there. It's just not a big thing.

Let's not let our imaginations get carried away, now, shall we?

CHAPTER 21

I wish I could say I was one of those people who just flops down on the bed and falls asleep at night. You know, a normal person. The kind of person who watches reruns of *Friends*. Or maybe is a big fan of Cracker Barrel. And this normal kind of person just falls happily to sleep, not a care in the world.

But, my dearest dears, I have never been that person. Not since I was a little stick with a mop of hair, looking not unlike a lollipop. I can't remember a time, or a place, where I did not flop on the bed, no matter how tired, and immediately start going through the catalog in my head of reasons for impending doom. I wish I had just been named Impending Doom. If I had just been named Impending

Doom, everyone would know what to expect.

The worker guys outside are cleaning up for the day. At this point I have a habit of waiting for the sound of hammers and drills to stop, then sneaking to the window and staring out from behind the lace curtains at each of them, unsuspecting, putting various screwdrivers and saws in their proper places. You learn a lot by watching people when they don't know they're being watched.

For instance, I notice that these guys don't feel nary an iota of shame walking around in a slump with their guts spilling out over their jeans. Not like girls.

No, it's too terrible. But these guys. Welp, they just let it all hang out. And another thing, this may sound weird—and it's quite possible I don't know anything about this, mind you—but it really does seem like they've been digging that hole for the foundation for an awfully long time. Like, the whole time. And every day I expect to wake up and see the beginnings of the guesthouse, but it's still, somehow, that same amount of dirt dug out of the ground. No change.

Is there some issue with the permits? Is there some issue with the ground? Maybe they accidentally dug into an electrical line? A water pipe? A water vein? What do you even call it? Is there even a way to measure it? To measure their lack of progress? For what? To report back to the professor. Yes, that's it. I must report their progress.

But then, wait. Am I then a snitch? Am I prepared to be a snitch?

Snitches get stitches.

That's weird. That just jumped into my head. How do I even know that expression? What am I? A hardened criminal? From C-block? (Whatever that is.)

I'm about to contemplate the intricacies of digging a foundation when—

BANG.

The screen door clanks in its frame from the direction of the pantry, and I feel a sudden draft of air.

I try to regain some sense of composure, but there is Mike, everyguy Mike, standing not two feet away from me. Quite frankly, a little too close. Where the heck did he come from?

I think the rule is . . . you announce yourself. Then, when the other person acknowledges you, you step forward and begin the conversation. This guy is a little too close. This guy is a space invader.

"Oh, hi. Yeah, no, I was just—"

(Spying on your friends.)

(Analyzing your digging progress.)

(Judging your rate of progress.)

"I was just—cleaning the window here."

He looks at me.

I don't have a sponge or a rag or nary a paper towel. I don't have window cleaner, or any kind of cleaner whatsoever in my hand or anywhere near me.

Normal Mike keeps staring at me.

Okay, this is just getting weird now.

Yes, I know I just made up the most ludicrous excuse of all time but, seriously, pipe up, mister!

He stays looking at me, his eyes almost a bit . . . I want to say . . . glassy. Maybe just kind of unfocused. Like he's looking at me but not looking at me. Almost like he's looking through me.

I gotta say, Mike is a pretty basic guy and this is definitely not basic behavior. We have left station stop Basic and gone straight to Weirdoville.

"Um . . . Mike?"

He stands there.

"Helloooooo. Anybody home? Mike? Earth to Mike? Come in, Mike?"

And yet nothing.

Alright, folks, now I am officially starting to get freaked out. Before, that was like a minor snafu. But this . . . this is getting a little into dead-eyed White Walker territory.

I take a tentative step backward and the sound of the floorboard, on a scale of one to ten of creaking is probably, I would say, at about a hundred.

CRee*eeeEEEEEAAAAK.*

Somehow the impossibly loud sound of the floorboards wakes him from his zombie state and he looks around him in confusion. Flustered.

"Um . . . hello? Are you okay? Mike?"

"What? Oh, um . . . I just. Wait. How'd I get in here?"

Well, this is strange.

I look behind him at the back door, ajar, by the pantry and point.

"Looks like that's probably how . . . seeing that the door is open." I try to make a joke but both of us are too confused to really feel the humor.

"No, but . . ." He scratches his head. "I was just . . . outside."

Now he's pointing to the backyard. The rest of the men seem to be gone and the only sound now is the screen door clattering up against the doorframe.

"Well, hmm. You're inside now, so . . ."

"Yeah, okay. Um. Sorry to bother you. Musta just—" He turns around to leave, embarrassed, "Musta just not drank enough water or something." He attempts a vague laugh.

"Oh, yeah. That's . . . I totally get it. Hydration is very important."

Yes, that was me who said that, sounding not unlike my kindergarten teacher.

"Well, I guess I'll see you next week. Have a good weekend!" He dashes off, giving an awkward little wave on his way out the door.

Weekend?

Who said anything about the weekend?

Is it really the weekend? I must have lost track of the date in my halcyon days of summer here.

Isn't the weekend supposed to illicit some sort of general elation? Like, "Oh, yeah, it's the weekend! Party time!"

But somehow that's not what I feel when I hear the word "weekend."

Nope. Not at all. When I hear the word "weekend," all I can think is . . .

Two days.

By myself.

CHAPTER 22

Can we all just admit that that was totally bizarre? I mean, first the guy comes in, swoops in, really . . . then he doesn't say anything. Not a word. Then, when he does say something, he doesn't even know how he got there.

Wait.

The thought hits me.

Maybe heeeeeeee is . . . on drugs.

Maybe that's his problem.

Maybe he's just a total stoner. Maybe he decided to start celebrating the weekend early and just lost track of the normal parameters of space and time.

It's not like that's the first time that's happened to a person.

I heard of a guy who smoked a bunch of LSD and then tried to fly. Jumped off a building! I know. Splat. Just like that. Gone-o.

So, maybe that's all it was with our dear Mike.

He seemed a little square to me, but never judge a book by its cover.

Also, that would account for the no-talky thing. How could he form words if he couldn't even figure out space and time?

And the glassy eyes.

I've heard that that happens, too.

So, you see. Again. Occam's razor. The simplest explanation is probably the correct one.

The guy was blotto.

These are the niceties I tell myself as I make my way to the kitchen to make my ever-so-nutritious ramen noodles out of the packet. Five for ninety-nine cents. You really can't beat that.

I know, I know. Please don't lecture me about kale or lettuce or quinoa. I just need some delicious yet easy-to-make comfort food. Something warm and simple to take up with me to the comfort of my bedroom as I space out watching the latest *Ancient Aliens* and fall asleep dreaming about the Sumerians and how their first leader was supposed to rule for thirty thousand years.

Simple stuff.

As is my wont, I fill the giant blue pot with water and light the stove. (It's gas; you have to light it. I know, annoying.) Then I place the pot of water on the burner and look through the cupboard for my ramen noodle packet, spicy chicken flavor.

Then, I turn back to the burner and this is when the world ends.

CHAPTER 23

Ladies and gentlemen of the jury, I would like to hereby assert that, under penalty of perjury, what I'm going to tell you now is absolutely, 100 percent true. There are no drugs involved, no booze, not even a chamomile tea.

And I know you're not going to believe me.

But I'm telling you.

I did not leave the room.

I did not even take more than a half step.

I was there the whole time.

Right there.

And . . . when I turn back to the burner where I *just put* the blue pot, which I *just filled* with water . . .

It's not there.

Oh, the burner is still going. That all is keeping up with reality.

But no pot.

And then . . . I look at the counter, look at the sink, look in my hands, for God's sake . . . and still no pot.

And then I see it.

Not casually set about, or happenstance over to the side, or asymmetrical in any way.

Nope.

Nope.

The pot, ladies and gentlemen of the jury, is . . .

Perfectly placed. Not an inch to the right or left.

Pristinely set.

In the middle of the kitchen floor.

CHAPTER 24

I know I know I know. It's just a pot. Right? I mean how could it mean anything? I get it.

But the problem is that there is no *physical* way in the universe that said pot could have moved. Nope. No way.

And the precision of it. It's so pristinely placed in the middle of the floor. You could measure it, from each side. The exact center.

This makes no sense.

I stare at the pot in the middle of the white kitchen tile floor.

What to do, what to do . . . ?

"Okay, self. You're basically staring in fear at a pot right now. I mean, get ahold of yourself. It's just . . . a . . . pot. We're just going to pretend that didn't happen. That somehow there is a logical explanation for this."

I know the next step but I don't want to say it.

"Daffodil, you have to just pick up the pot now . . . act like everything's normal . . . and put it back on the stove. That's it. This is not rocket science."

I exhale. I remind myself that this is just kitchenware.

But . . . my feet remain glued to the ground.

Drastic measures are needed.

"IT'S JUST KITCHENWARE!" I yell into the floor, the sound echoing off the ceiling and the white octagon tiles.

And now I just go.

Grab the pot.

Put it back on the burner.

Stare at the pot.

A watched pot never boils.

Also, a watched pot never magically puts itself in the center of the floor.

That's my new motto.

I stand there for about three thousand years, watching the water in the pot taking forever to boil.

But I am watching this damn pot.

I better keep myself company.

"Well, what are you going to watch tonight, Daffodil? . . .

I don't know, self, I was thinking about watching the Silk Road series or maybe that other flat-earther doc or maybe the new *Ancient Aliens* . . . Yes, self, that sounds like a plan! . . . Yes, self, indeed. *Ancient Aliens* it is!"

Have I had this conversation before? This is all seeming strangely familiar.

Finally, the watched-pot water boils, in defiance of the phrase, and the unhealthy ramen noodle dinner begins.

I could stay here in the kitchen that obviously has some sort of pot portal going on . . . or I could just eat this upstairs, while I contemplate the pyramids, the Hopi people, and the Aztecs. As if this is any real choice. Why would I care about a mysteriously guided pot when there are such bigger things to blow my mind. Like the fact that, I mean, maybe those pyramids are actually some sort of electromagnetic energy device. Mind blown.

I put the strange-minded pot into the "don't think about" folder on my brain desktop. Then I click over to it, drag it into the trash, and empty the trash right there.

Done.

See?

Easy as pie.

I'm just about to happily, calmly, peacefully march up the stairs when I hear the crisp sound of an English accent cutting through the air.

"Hallo? Toodle-oo!"

To my infinite annoyance, Penelope is already in the hall-way, heading into the kitchen.

I want to tell her to actually knock, or, say, maybe give me a little notice, but she is already barreling past any such qualms.

"Oh dear, when was the last time you had a proper meal, dear girl?"

"Um . . ."

"Quite right. Here, let's see what we have here in these cupboards. . . ."

"Uh, you know I was just—"

"A knife, I need a knife . . ." she mutters to herself, look-ing around.

"It seems like, perhaps maybe you could—"

"Found it!" She turns to me now, chipper, which would be fine except for the fact that she now has a rather large butcher knife in her hand.

"Um, to be honest, I'm really not that—"

"Hungry?" she says, still chipper.

But there is something strange in her smile. Something sideways and falling off to the left. A bright smile, but uncer-tain.

And the butcher knife. In her hand. Gleaming.

"Do you mind if we just, uh, call it a day. I'm really uh . . ."

"Oh! Is this not a good time then?" The smile begins to falter, sliding off her lips.

"Well, it's just . . . it's just—"

"Oh, it's fine, dear. I know when I'm not wanted. Quite fine." And this passive-aggressive turn now made menacing by the butcher knife, still in hand.

I want to shout, "Hand over the butcher knife!" but, of course, I can't. Or I don't.

"You know . . . little girls like you all alone in a house like this. It's not right. I mean, think! Anything could happen to you."

Butcher knife still in hand.

When the hell is she going to put it down?

"Deary, you simply can't be here by yourself. It's not safe." She comes closer now. Seeming almost to glide.

"Excuse me, I . . ." And now I'm light-headed, not knowing what to do. Suddenly she's transformed, and seems so menacing. So close. Still holding the gleaming knife.

"I'm afraid for you, my darling! I'm afraid for you, here, in this place! You don't know what could happen! What has occurred!"

And now she's suddenly short of breath, panicked, mania in her eyes, still holding the knife.

"Please, you just need to sit down. Perhaps some water . . ."
And I turn toward the refrigerator, but just as I turn, I see
her out of the corner of my eye. . . .

She lunges!

She lunges toward me with the knife.

It splits the air, gleaming, an arc down, right where my
back was just a split second ago!

"Jesus!" I hurl myself to the other side of the room, but
now she is . . . she is something else . . . a decrepit, deranged
thing, heading toward me, throwing herself toward me.

And I fucking run.

I fling myself into the hallway and up the stairs, not
knowing what I am doing until I do it.

"No, no! There is method to my madness! You will see!
Let me show you!"

Looking back in glances, I see with horror that she is now
not the sweet old lady from somewhere posh in England,
but a haggard, kind of shriveled shrew following me, spout-
ing maniacally about the house.

"It's this house! Don't you see?! The house does it to
everyone! It will do it to you! That's why, this is why! You
must be gone before it's too late!"

And again, she catapults herself toward me, swinging the
knife in the motion of a sickle, and I'm not even touching
the ground now, just hurling myself forward, just seeming

to fly upward and away, thinking, *think, Daffodil,* thinking what can I do, how can I make this stop. She is mad! She is truly mad!

And the thought in a thunderclap . . . who the hell is this lady . . . who is she? The professor never introduced her. *She* said she was a friend. That was *her* report. *She* could have come from anywhere, from the town, from the street, some homeless woman from Philadelphia, possibly wandered in from the city . . . and I'm breathless, I'm panicking. . . .

"Dear, it's not you, no, no, it's the house!!" And with that she plunges the knife, meant for me, into the stair just beneath me and . . . at the very same moment, I hurl the chinoiserie vase at her head. It lands with a crack on her skull and then falls down the stairs, breaking into a hundred pieces, and in the silence, then, she is left, staring up at me with horrified eyes.

I stand there on the top of the third-floor landing, as a drop of blood comes down from her orange hat, followed by a streamlet, then a stream. Her eyes are fixed on me, startled, but then, something else . . . a glimmer of something, almost a smile.

"You see, deary . . ." The blood is now dripping down over her blouse, her skirt, onto the floor. ". . . it's the house."

And with that she stutter-steps backward, and that step is too faulty, too uneven, to keep her, but in a moment there, she seems suspended in the air, with that half smile and that blood coming down. And then down she falls backward, over the chinoiserie vase shards, over herself, into the railing.

Onto the landing below.

CHAPTER 25

I stand there now, at the top of the landing, looking over the banister, frozen.

Below me, on the second-floor landing, is a crumpled mass of filthy, disheveled, mismatched patterns now splotched in blood, a new pattern, a blotch pattern, and the body, inanimate, the orange hat, displaced, and a stream of blood making its way across the floorboards, heading toward the rug. A Persian rug, probably worth a fortune.

What did I just do?

I can't even say the words. Or think the thought.

Did that just happen?

But clearly it did.

I mean, look at her. There she is, for all the world to see, splayed out on the parquet floor.

Jesus Christ.

No, not a swear word. Really, just . . . Jesus Christ. Help me. What do I do? What have I done?

Okay, this happened to me once before. I remember . . . Grandma was teaching me how to drive, and a man ran out into the road, and I had to swerve, and we almost crashed into a wooden pole, but then I turned just in time, and we were fine, and and and . . . I just had to do deep breaths . . . and count back from ten . . .

Ten. Nine. Eight. Yes, breath. Seven. Six. Slow it down. Five. Four. There you go. Three. Two . . . One.

Daffodil. Calm down.

You can do this.

I take a moment to assess.

Okay.

This is bad. Yes, solve the problems. Take them in order.

What is the immediate problem?

Exhale.

The immediate problem is there is a dead body on the landing.

A dead body that you put there.

You are a murderer.

Okay, back to one.

Exhale.

Let's think about this for a second. In every *Law & Order* you have ever watched, the murderer panics. This is the moment they start to make all sorts of panicked decisions. This is the moment they screw up.

I will not screw this up.

It was not my fault. Right?

It was self-defense.

The knife is no longer in her hand, but it's next to her on the landing.

That means . . . there will be fingerprints. That will prove it was self-defense.

Don't move anything.

Leave it just as it is. Call 911.

That's it!

Call 911!

You were only defending yourself.

Let the cops come, be honest. Don't move anything.

I tiptoe backward, searching for my phone, which I *always* lose, I swear to God. Where is it?

It's not on the bed, it's not on the bedside table.

Don't think about what's below, just concentrate on the phone, Daffodil.

Maybe it's in the bathroom, check over there. . . .

No, it's not in the bathroom, maybe back in the bedroom, maybe it fell on the floor—

Wait.

I catch a glimpse.

Wait.

What the . . . ?

No.

No no no no no.

It can't be.

It's out of the corner of my eye that I see it. I want to tell myself it's not there. I want to try to keep my head on straight. Just fasten it on.

But there it is.

Now I turn.

I turn fully toward it.

I turn fully toward it and it envelops me.

CHAPTER 26

If you were me, you would be standing at the top of the third-floor landing in a beautiful old house, hyperventilating.

If you were me, you would be looking down at the second-floor landing, where you would be seeing something you could not quite comprehend.

If you were me, you would be, at this moment, convinced that perhaps you had lost your faculties.

Because what is on that landing is much worse than anything you could imagine.

Because what is on that landing is . . .

Nothing.

. . .

There is nothing on that landing now at all.

No crumpled flower fabric, no blood seeping down, no body curled in on itself, no chinoiserie shards, no gleaming butcher knife.

Nothing.

The only thing worse than what was there is now what isn't there.

Okay, let's start this again.

Exhale. Three. Two. One.

"Daffodil." I say my name. Maybe somehow my name can ground me.

I begin to look around and, again, a start, when I see, next to me, on the side table . . . oh please God . . . please God, what is happening . . .

On the side table.

The chinoiserie vase.

Standing upright.

Back in one piece now.

The room is seeming to spin now to dizzying heights as my calming breaths seem not to hold me and my knees decide to buckle.

The floor can be hard or it can be soft—in this moment, it's nonexistent because everything turns to black before I hit it.

CHAPTER 27

The morning light is coming through the curtains in golden, dusty streams, lighting up the floorboards beneath me.

Yes, I am still on the third-floor landing.

I'm just about to remember what put me here, what happened the night before, when I hear a voice I haven't heard since early spring. A voice in a whisper.

The voice seems like it's coming in with the dawn light, as if sent from the same golden place, gilded with hope and kindness.

"Daffodil . . . you must remember."

Squinting into the sunlight, again, in a whisper, "Remember . . . remember me."

The words like a hand reaching out, beckoning, kind, forgiving.

But the voice is unmistakable.

I know that voice. I'd know that voice anywhere. The way that voice says my name. The caress in it.

And a tear comes to my eye, just hearing that voice, that voice I miss with every cell in my body.

That voice.

Zander.

I look up into the sunlight, the hope streaming in, trying to follow the voice. I catch my balance, get up, and make my way into the light coming in, hoping to hear it again.

"Zander?" It's a desperate plea, held in a whisper.

Maybe this is the whisper of a madwoman.

A madwoman who murders people on the stairs.

"Zander? Is that you . . . ?" I look up into the light coming in, but something has ended, something has passed, and nothing answers.

It's gone.

That voice.

That hope.

That question.

What is it? What is it I'm supposed to remember? Or is this just a dream, too?

I'm getting so confused now. What is a dream and what

is real? What if I put them down? Put them in a column.

Okay, okay.

Let's just sit down now. Let's just sit down. And think.

I don't bother going down the steps. I can't. I can't go down there yet.

And, also, this sounds strange, I know. But there's something keeping me up here. Something in this morning light. Just like the doctor said! Morning light. Daffodil, you must get morning light.

Easy now.

Sit down and let's figure.

What is the most logical explanation for what is happening here?

What do we know?

We know you're staying in this house. We know the professor is counting on you to watch over the construction. We know you're getting paid. A lot.

We also know . . . that you are having bad dreams. Viciously bad dreams. Nightmares. Like the unspeakable nightmare from last night. When you killed someone. But, Daffodil, you did not kill anyone.

That, too, was a dream.

Just like the desolate-house dream.

And now, I console myself. Daffodil . . . you've always had vivid dreams. You're very good at it. Always have been.

What is probably happening . . . if I were my shrink I would say this. What is probably happening is that you are under a lot of stress, with all the changes, with leaving home, with going off to college, with the unspeakable-thing-that-shall-remain-nameless. Perhaps, even, with your ideas of self-destruction. Perhaps this is a kind of defense.

Maybe, even, with the prospect of hurling yourself in front of a Mack truck, your subconscious is giving you things to be scared of. Things to make you realize that, ultimately, you actually *don't* want to die. That, confronted with the reality of death . . . say, someone lunging at you with a butcher knife . . . you actually want to live. That you must live. (That you would kill to live, but don't think that. It's too horrible.)

A diagnosis.

Stress. Transition. Self-preservation.

My own mind is playing tricks on me to get me to admit that I want to live, I want to go to college, I want to go to Bryn Mawr. I want to survive. I do not want to throw away my life. Maybe I just want, desperately, to change it.

A revelation.

"Daffodil. Face it. You love this world. In your own weird way. It makes you curious." I'm muttering to myself on the bed. "You love learning. You love strange facts. You love contemplating empires and the fall of empires and ancient aliens and Sumerians and the Silk Road. And, despite yourself, you actually want to live."

A calm comes over me now.

It's okay. There's a diagnosis. There's a reason.

All is well.

I feel light now.

As if a weight is lifted.

My lie to myself.

No, I'm not going to hurl myself at a moving vehicle.

I refuse.

There I am, about to gather myself for the day in a rational, normal way, when I hear the sound of a car winding up the long drive.

It's a bit early, but nobody seems to care about that much around these parts.

I go to the window and stare out beneath me, down to the driveway, where a yellow SUV parks just in front of the house, awfully close.

Curious.

Perhaps this is the professor, come home early. I don't remember seeing his car . . . but this could be his. Although, I would peg him more for a Prius, quite frankly.

The door opens and the very tan leg of a very tan woman pokes out. Okay, definitely not the professor.

It's a kind of orange spray tan, I remember well from

some of the country club girls back in Nebraska. It's not really a color the sun would ever make you. Unless the sun hated you.

Now the hair pokes out. This hair is did. A fresh blowout, stick straight. Blond. Quite long, actually. And the outfit is did, too. Put together. Buttoned up.

A kind of skirt suit, pencil skirt, blazer, matching in a dark teal. This lady is really going for it. Officious.

She looks up at the house, and I jump backward, frantic.

There is zero way I am interacting with this woman.

I mean, what the heck would I even say? Nice blazer? What's your favorite gym? How do you get such an allover tan that definitely isn't orange?

Before I can imagine the hundreds of awkward sentences I could say to her, she grabs a clipboard and begins walking around the house.

A clipboard?

What is that even for?

Do people even make those anymore?

But there she is, clipboard in hand, heels in the dirt, walking around the house and seeming to make notes to herself.

Okaaaaaaay.

I suppose I should probably go down there.

Should being the operative word.

I have a good excuse, though. I think you will agree.

I murdered someone last night.

Or, at least, I think I did.

So . . . it's not exactly the best timing. I mean, I don't think it's a stretch to say this is not the ideal time for an interaction with someone who would be painful for me to interact with in the first place.

No, no. The proper thing to do is to just hide in the attic.

I mean, what harm could she do? She's wearing coral lipstick.

If you think I am going to follow her to the back of the house, you are correct. I am going to spy on her every move because we have established that this is one of my favorite hobbies.

Man, she is really in shape. I can even see her calf muscles from up here. That is some serious keto and Pilates right there. Her walk is brilliant, it's so confident.

Funny thing, about that walk, she now seems to be taking it inside the house.

Now, that's confidence.

I know, I know. I should do something. I should say something.

But, again, I have social anxiety. And this lady, welp, she is like the poster child for *why* I have social anxiety.

I bet if I looked in the mirror, I would scream.

No no no. I simply cannot.

One thing I can do, though, is peek out over the banister and see what she's up to.

But maybe I should protect. I should protect the hearth and home of the professor!

She enters and stands in the entryway and promptly sneezes. She gathers herself and begins writing notes.

Okay, this is getting weird. I sort of have to do something . . . which is my least favorite sentence.

But, okay, here goes.

"Um, hellooooo, can I help you?"

I don't descend the stairs because, honestly, I really don't want her to see me. I don't want anyone to see me in my current state, but especially not her.

She replies in a sneeze.

Hmm. A summer cold. Unusual but not unheard of.

"Hello? Is there something I can help you with . . . ?"

ACHOO!

I'm about to raise my voice, for the last time, but as providence would have it . . . she sneezes again. And again. And again. And hallelujah! She sneezes her way right out the front door, back into her yellow SUV, down the driveway, and all the way down the road. *Achoo! Achoo! ACHOO!*

I love it.

I love it!

See, this is such a weird world.

Sometimes you just have to stick around to see what strange thing is going to happen.

And the best part about it is . . . I didn't even have to talk to anyone!

Praise Jesus.

CHAPTER 28

The rest of the day is uneventful.

I take this day easy, I'm light on myself. I go for a walk in the sun. I read my latest book, about the loss of a yellow house in Katrina. I contemplate all the different things I may or may not do in a hurricane. I take a bath, I get into bed, Normal von Borington.

Everything is just light now.

The calm after the storm.

And I'm actually chipper.

(I think part of this is the relief, the enormous relief, of knowing that I didn't kill anyone. Boy, that'll take a load off your shoulders.)

Drifting off to sleep, I remember the absolute best thing

ever to happen to anyone and that someone happened to be me.

And, yes, it involves Zander Haaf.

The heart of my everything.

Last time we were pondering him he had just emptied the seat next to him in Biology 101 and was writing notes to me in a heated manner. Just for me. Strange, unpopular me!

As we know, this is not exactly how things were supposed to be at my high school. I'm too eccentric, and by that I mean odd, and by that I mean weird.

So, Zander Haaf is not supposed to be making a special effort, or any effort, whatsoever, my way.

I mean, if I were a cheerleader . . . maybe.

But I'm not really cheerleader material.

If there was like a depressionleader . . . that I could qualify for. I could probably fill the whole depressionleader squad.

Instead of wearing those little skirts and jumping around everywhere, we would wear all black and slink all over ourselves. We wouldn't have cheers so much as moans. And our patented move would be . . . the eye roll.

But I digress . . . back to Zander Haaf.

Sometime, as I'm peering into my biology book as a way to hide, another little note appears by my elbow.

I look at it.

Zander gestures to me, looking around suspiciously.

I decide to pick up the note.

I now look back at Zander, who gives me an encouraging nod. For some reason, this time, I decide to actually open the note.

It says:

Do you like circles or squares?

I look up at him. Ah, he's making fun of me. But he gestures at me to write back.

Um . . . okay.

Maybe I will.

I fold over the paper and write on the other side.

Neither of them appeal to me. I like triangles.

And then, he takes the note. Reads it. Thinks. And writes again.

If you could have a warthog, a pig, or a guinea pig . . . which would you choose?

I pick up the note. Think. And write back.

Is there going to be a test?

He reads it, smiles, and shrugs.

I take the note back and write:

Definitely a guinea pig. But I already have two bunnies and a dog.

He looks at me, tilting his head, then writes again:

What are their names?

And I write back:

The bunnies are named Star Performer and Hammy.

The dog is named Sandwich.

He looks at the paper and stifles a laugh, not wanting to attract the attention of Mr. Eckdahl.

Then I look at him and make some sort of non-sign language gesture for "Stop writing me notes. We're going to get in trouble!" . . . pointing back at Mr. Eckdahl.

He nods, and then does a mock respectful salute.

After a few minutes of pretending to read from my textbook, I muster up the courage to look at him.

He smiles and waves his finger at me, then does the shush gesture, finger to his lips, mocking me. Like now he's telling me to behave. When I was the one who told him!

I roll my eyes, but I know what my face is doing. My face is blushing.

My face is blushing and all my cells are blushing and my whole body is blushing. And I am going to have to hide in my textbook because I can't stand to look at him. I can't bear it. It makes too many things happen to me. It shakes everything up. It throws me off my game. (Not that I have any game.) But it makes me feel giddy and scared and dizzy.

And I can't take it.

CHAPTER 29

In the dead of night, something much less cheerful happens.

I hesitate to tell you because it might sound crazy or, worse, make me go back to seeming a little insane.

But I'm pretty sure it happened.

Not bet-a-million-dollars sure.

But kind of sure.

I think it must have been around three or four in the morning. The quietest time. Some people call it the witching hour.

But this doesn't involve a witch.

Nope.

This just involves me waking up in a haze, staring at the ceiling, and a thought . . . not a thought, really. But more like words, spoken to me . . . in my head. In a voice I've never heard. A man's voice. Deep.

So not my thought.

Someone else's thought.

Given to me.

And the thought is . . .

The voice whispers . . .

"Get the hammer."

CHAPTER 30

Mornings are supposed to be quiet and peaceful. Birds are supposed to chirp and the sun is supposed to cast everything in gold.

But this morning isn't quiet because this morning there is a horrible knocking, a rude sort of knocking, on the front door downstairs. Almost banging.

It's the last thing you want to hear when you're bleary-eyed and sweaty and disheveled and confused. It means: You have to get up, out of your warm, snuggly bed, and go downstairs and interact with whoever is banging away down there. Loud enough to wake the devil himself. And all his minions.

"Greetings! Toodle-oo!" It's Penelope. Penelope Persephone Crisp. There on the porch, banging on the door.

Oh God.

The last time I saw this person, I murdered this person.

Okay, but I didn't.

I didn't.

Obviously.

Because here she is!

So, really, I should just act normal. Because nothing happened.

Again, Daffodil, repeat after me.

None. Of. That. Happened.

Just calm down.

Quite frankly, I find myself both annoyed and comforted by her unexpected presence. Again, there's not a word for that. Annforted. Comfannoyed?

Yes, I'm comfannoyed.

But her presence does substantiate the fact that I did not kill her. I think we can all agree, this is a bonus.

"Is anyone home? Helloooo?" She peers through the little glass window, her perky orange hat perched atop her head.

"Coming! Yes, I'm here!" I lug my slug self down the stairs and to the front, opening the door.

"Oh, dear. Did I wake you?" She adds, "You look dreadful."

"Thanks. Yes. I'm not really a morning person," I say, a not-so-subtle hint to never come over this early.

"Well, you know what they say, the early bird gets the worm!"

"And, also, no sleep . . . so it really should be 'the early bird gets no sleep.'"

She looks at me, mock reproachful. "Oh, you! Well, you are clever, I'll give you that. No wonder they let you into Bryn Mawr. You know, I have two cousins who went to Vassar, a niece who went to Radcliffe, a granddaughter who just graduated from Mount Holyoke, and another granddaughter who will be attending Smith in the fall. Almost all the Seven Sisters seem to be represented! No Barnard, yet, however. I don't know quite why that is. Quite a campus there, you know. . . ."

As she's giving this Seven Sisters promotional speech she glides around the room, taking off her hat, dusting off a few books, readjusting a pastoral painting of some kind of autumnal hunt, and then sitting down in a wingback chair.

I can't help marveling at her assumption of being welcome. Yes, she is welcome . . . but would it kill her to ask at least?

Don't say kill her. Keep "kill" and "her" in different sentences, Daffodil.

"I'll bet you haven't had one proper meal since you've been staying here, have you?" She looks at me. "Tell me, what have you been eating, dear girl?"

I don't like where this is going. Last time we had this conversation it ended in homicide.

"Um . . . mostly ramen noodles," I admit.

"Dreadful. We shall have to fix that. Do you have any money? I could give you some," she suggests.

"Oh God, no. I couldn't take it. I'm fine really." Even the suggestion somehow fills me with shame.

But now she is looking somewhere else. "That's strange."

Dread rolls down my spine, a cold wave. The tone shift. From Mary Poppins to one of Macbeth's witches. This has happened before. Is it happening again? I follow her eye to where she is looking.

"Didn't there use to be a frog in there?" She peers at the jar of murky liquid on the shelf.

The empty jar.

Wait.

What?

Why is the jar empty?

"Where is the frog?" She says my exact thought out loud. "It's clearly not in there."

She turns to me.

Wait . . . does she think I took the frog?

"Um . . . I have no idea where the frog is. That's the weirdest thing. I mean . . ." I utter.

This is officially becoming a very confusing morning.

"Well, it couldn't have just leapt out of its jar and closed the lid behind it now, could it?"

And she's right. Of course.

How the heck did that frog get out of there? Is this some kind of prank?

"Did . . . you . . . take it out?" I ask her.

"Me! Now, why on earth would I do such a thing? Absurd!"

And it is absurd.

It's absurd to be pondering the existence of a frog but it is also absurd that a frog could just disappear out of its murky display jar.

"Be honest. Did you take it?" She tilts her head.

"No! Of course not! Why would I?! I don't even like things like that . . . frogs in jars, animals on the wall, taxidermy . . . it all just seems kind of gross, honestly."

She peers at me over her wire-rim glasses, seeming to size me up.

Then she makes a judgment.

"No. No, you don't seem the type."

I nod. "Thank you. Geez. I'm not, like, some psychopath."

"Of course not, dear. No one is saying that. But it is a bit odd, don't you think?"

"Yeah . . . I mean, yes. It's . . . completely . . . bizarre." I walk to the jar, inspecting it closer. The lid is perfectly in place. I try the lid and not only is it in place, but it's actually tight. "This is so strange."

"Indeed," she agrees. "But after all, it is just a frog, isn't it?" She comforts me in her very English way.

"Yes, right. Just a frog." I don't want to seem like an absolute nitwit, so I agree.

"May I suggest something, dear?" She leans in.

"Sure. Yes. Of course."

"Why don't you go for a little walk down the road into town, shop around a little bit, maybe pick up a book, maybe have tea at that sweet little café there?"

Tea. Why are the Brits so obsessed with tea? Anything happens . . . "Put the kettle on." A death in the family. "Put the kettle on." Tornado. "Put the kettle on." Nuclear war. "Put the kettle on."

"It might be nice to get out a little, don't you think? This house is beautiful, but it can be . . . a bit isolated, yes?" she suggests.

It's surprisingly kind, coming from her. Not that she's unkind. She's just so . . . English.

"Yes, good idea. I should," I think out loud.

"I can accompany you part of the way, my dear, but then I'm afraid I have to run a little errand just over the hill there."

"No, it's fine. It's okay. I just . . . do you mind waiting?" I realize what I look like. "I can't exactly go like this."

"Of course, dear." She settles back in the chair and picks up a dusty book from the end table, blowing off a bit of the dust. She reads the title, "A *Comprehensive History of the Silk Road.*"

"Hmm," I say, meaning nothing. But inside I am thinking, I have heard this before, too. Where have I heard it?

It's strange that this very book would be there, now. A book I hadn't noticed but that I would certainly have noticed, as it falls firmly in the realm of my imagination.

"Fascinating. I always do love hearing the tales of the ancient world. Palmyra. The Assyrians. The Phoenicians and their many trade routes along the Mediterranean." She squints a little, a gesture of intrigue.

"I do, too. I'm obsessed, actually," I admit. "One day, I want to travel the Silk Road. Maybe even on the back of a camel. See Palmyra. The ruins of Turpan."

"Pity it's all devastated these days. I should like to visit, too, one day," she confesses, wistful.

"Oh, I'm sure you'll get to see it," I assure her.

"Not at my age, dear. I can only imagine it these days, through documentaries and the like. I couldn't possibly go. Can you imagine me in a war zone?" She laughs it off.

And it is a bit sad, isn't it? The idea that all these grand treasures, secrets, and mysteries, the cradle of civilization between the Tigris and the Euphrates, is now essentially on fire. A whole world of treasures ablaze. As if we're setting fire to ourselves.

"One day, when you have children of your own, I hope you look them right in the eye and tell them wars are nothing more than rich men sending poor men to die killing other poor men." She says this, suddenly wistful, as if she knows quite a bit more about it. More than she's willing to tell.

But, again, something about her tells me she has seen everything. Perhaps she's seen the kinds of things you would spend your whole life trying to forget.

I duck out, making my way up the stairs, hurrying to get dressed, not wanting to be rude.

Downstairs I can hear her humming a little song to herself. I don't recognize the song, or the lyrics, but there is something consoling in it.

A melancholy song, sung to only herself:

"You'll never know just how much I miss you . . .

You'll never know just how much I care. . . ."

I stand there on the landing for a minute, not knowing why, wondering who it is Penelope would be singing this song for.

"You went away and my heart went with you . . .

I speak your name in my every prayer."

Strange, isn't it? That Penelope, too, must have that some-one. That someone you see when you close your eyes. That someone you're still with even though you're not.

Like being haunted.

Which is the same as being in love.

CHAPTER *31*

We're about a fifth of the way down the winding road when Penelope veers off to the right down a smaller path, saying a few kind words and a polite "Toodle-oo."

Yes, my dream about her was terrifying. Yes, she has a tendency to enter whenever she pleases, wake me up too early, and say rude things out of the blue. But there's no one else around here I can even think about speaking to. My condition, such as it is, is too debilitating. Perhaps someone else would have someone to help—a parent, a friend. But I'm fresh out of those.

And so, by virtue of the fact that she seems to feel entitled to interaction with me, she has it.

Which somehow reminds me of Zander. He insisted on my attention, my response.

He insisted on that argument that night. Wouldn't stop because we *had to talk*.

No, not that. Don't think about that.

This is supposed to be a morning of merrily strolling along, getting some fresh air and a new perspective.

I am supposed to be listening to the birds chirping and the bees buzzing, and enjoying the warmth of the sun on my face.

I resolve to spend the rest of my pastoral walk singing random songs and admiring the wildflowers on the side of the road.

"You went away and my heart went with you . . .

I speak your name in my every prayer."

I always think one day I'm going to become an expert on flora and fauna, the type of person who can simply look at a plant and know its name by heart . . . but I never do it.

Maybe that's what I could do. Buy a book on each flower and plant, memorize them, and then impress everyone with my extensive knowledge of the natural world!

Ah, yes, that must be an agave attenuata!

Oh, would you look at that willow acacia?

Ah, is that a red-tip photinia?!

Okay, that sounds more like a bird. But maybe that will

be the next step. Bird knowledge. I'll be a bird-watcher. A birder. A person who can simply hear the sound of a specific chirp and say, "Why that must be a black-throated green warbler! Oh, do you hear the mockingbird? Listen? Do you hear his many various songs?"

Somehow this fantasy of myself involves a lot of khaki.

Not exactly my color.

Maybe I'll be a birder who wears black and hides in the bushes. Or the night. Maybe I'll be an owler!

No one can stop me.

I laugh to myself and my fantasy future. My ability to fantasize an entire scene, an entire future . . . like a tonic. I learned how to do this when my mom left. Taught myself to.

There was never any dad around and that was just the way it was. Other kids had a dad but somehow mine was missing. Maybe he was magical. Maybe he was a spy. An international spy who traveled the world and foiled bad guys. I would picture him chasing the villain through Red Square, or Paris, or Prague. In my imagination, he was always dashingly handsome. A sweep of jet-black hair and enormous dark eyes. A movie star.

And my mom, I didn't have to imagine, because she was right there with me. When I was little, little. I remember her long wheat-colored hair and her gray eyes, looking down at me, while she sang little songs. She was the lead star. The main attraction. When she was there my life was a movie and she was the beginning, the middle, and the end.

There is not an actress on this earth who could compare to her.

In my memory.

But then, one day, a strange thing happened. It was a gray March day, and when she was picking me up from my grandmother's house, she slipped on the ice. No big deal. Happens all the time. It's Nebraska.

But it was painful, her back somehow twisted in the fall. I remember her reaching her arm back and trying to squeeze the pain away. Standing there in the kitchen, on the linoleum floor, white and black checks.

Then she went to the doctor and, for a while after that, she was fine. Happy as a clam. Cheery even.

There were little plastic amber bottles with prescriptions all around the house. With strange names. Long, unpronounceable names.

And the doctor kept her from trying to squeeze the pain out of her back. The pills did that. The pills made everything better.

And then there were more and more pills and more and more plastic amber bottles. And sometimes she'd leave me at Grandma's so she could go to the doctor. And, at first, she'd just leave me for hours. But then she'd leave me the whole day. Then overnight. Then, for days.

And when she'd bring me home it was a strange home, a messy home, like a truck drove through it . . . clothes on the ground and nothing picked up and the bathroom smelling like piss and nothing clean. Nothing ever clean, nothing ever organized. But the pills. She always knew where the make-everything-better pills were. That part was organized.

And the pills made her happy! Happy happy smiles! Happy happy pills! And mom was back! My lead actress with the blond, blond hair was back! And I had her! And she loved me again! And we could be happy! We could be happy here, just mommy and me, together!

It was a Halloween party.

She was supposed to take me to.

I was the little mermaid.

Ariel.

Grandma had bought my outfit and even sewn on extra sequins for my sparkly green tail. And I had a long red wig that Grandma said made me look beautiful, and I couldn't wait for Mommy to see it. When she picked me up, she would see it. Couldn't she get here? Why wasn't she here already?

The lights all around the neighborhood were going on, the porch lights, and some even had orange twinkling lights, spooky decorations. A skeleton, a witch, a jack-o-lantern. Ghosts, hanging from the mailbox. And I couldn't wait wait wait to get out there. It's Halloween night!

"See! Grandma! Those kids are already trick-or-treating!"

"Be patient, honey. She'll be here."

But that "She'll be here" started sounding more and more strained and, every once in a while, my grandma would make her way to the kitchen where I could hear her pick up the phone and speak in hushed tones, whispering, frantic.

I just wanted her to see that I was Ariel! I was beautiful Ariel with the long red hair and sparkling green tail!

But . . . she never came.

She never came that night, with the pumpkins and the ghosts and the candy that all the other little kids had but now I didn't want. Couldn't have kept down, even if I'd tried. She never came even to that next pumpkin holiday, that Thanksgiving, even though Grandma set a plate for her. Empty next to the turkey. She never came even though Santa came, and Grandma made sure to leave out cookies and milk because she told me I'd been so good, such a good, good girl.

And she never came back.

This is a memory that I have but that I put far, far away. Off in Red Square or Paris or Prague. I paint over this memory with everything my mind can muster, oil paints and watercolors and wild sculptures that become real. Real things in my head that begin to move around on their own. And these real things, real things I imagined, they get to replace that red Ariel wig and that sparkly green tail. These now-real things get to protect me. To warm me. I wrap them around me like a blanket.

The little town reveals itself around the bend, tiny little boxes placed just so. From here, far away, they could be decoration models on a train set. A sweet little town the train *choo-choos* around at Christmas.

I make my way all the way up the road and into the quaint café. Opening the door, I realize I'm just not used to seeing that many people all at once. Not only that, but I get the distinct feeling everyone just recoiled from me. They didn't, actually, but I feel a change in the air.

Does everyone feel like this? Unwanted? Queasy at the thought of interaction? Or is this just me?

The eternal question.

Am I weird?

I make my way to a small table in the corner, because small tables in the corner are my natural habitat.

What am I even doing here, in this place? With that house and all its . . . what should we call them? Quirks?

I know what you're thinking.

Why haven't I googled it.

Right?

I mean . . . I'm staying there. Wouldn't anyone in their right mind google the address?

But I have an answer for you, *mon ami*. I have a very good reason not to have googled it because, you see, I am a very practical person and the logic goes like this: I have to stay there all summer, no matter what. That's the job. And the job is the only way I have to pay my freshman year room and board. So, if I don't stay there, then I can't go to college. And if I don't go to college, then I have to go back to Nebraska.

And that is not acceptable.

Then I certainly will hurl myself off the nearest bridge.

Two women in pastel-flower prints gab away about one of their grandchildren and his insistence on playing hours and hours of Roblox and how her daughter is a fool to let her son turn his brain into oatmeal like that. This continues through all the dreaded video games that are corroding the minds of our youth. *Minecraft*. Roblox. *Fortnite*. *Fortnite* really seems to be the one freaking them out.

I pretend to study the menu up behind the counter in chalk on a black chalkboard. I guess they must change it every day. I see they're out of split pea soup. That one is scribbled off.

I have never studied a menu so meticulously before.

Eggs. Scrambled. Hearty breakfast plate. Orange juice.

Waffles. Pancakes. Flapjacks. What's the difference between a flapjack and a pancake, anyway? Under the "Healthy Options" banner: Egg white scramble. Cottage cheese and fruit. Blech.

I notice something strange on the menu and let out a small laugh.

Frogs' legs.

I know, I know, it's absurd. Yes, there is a tiny piece of my brain that is wondering if the frog could have somehow, magically, been taken out of the jar back at the house, and is now on the menu. But that's ridiculous.

I feel like I'm losing my mind. The waitress is chatting away with a not-so-bad-looking guy in a trucker hat. I mean, he's not like a supermodel or anything . . . but for here . . . this place . . . pretty good.

That's a funny thing I noticed, on the train out here from my sweet little hick town to the outskirts of Philadelphia . . . the looks get progressively less ruddy as you go east. The faces get more sallow, the noses get thinner, and the circles under the eyes get purple. I know it seems an odd thing, but there are a lot of people back home with parents from all those cold climes up north in the Old World. Names of my old classmates . . . things like Hesse, Krauss, Meier. First names like Lars, Svan, and Uli. I guess that's just where they went to. Iowa. Wisconsin. Nebraska. Minnesota.

Maybe somehow those cold, punishing, below-zero winters and piles of snow felt like home to them. While everyone else scattered to sunnier climes.

And so everyone from Lincoln, Palmyra, and Kearney look sort of like extras in *The Sound of Music*. Von Trapp children. Von Trapp people. And now, getting closer to the east side of this continent, everyone looks more like the people you see on TV. Or in film. Not everyone has blond hair and a name like Lars.

I wave at the waitress. She doesn't seem to be in any big hurry to serve me and suddenly I find this annoying. What's her problem? Has she pegged me as an out-of-towner?

When I worked at the Runza, we were expected to immediately shout out "Welcome to Runza, a meal in a bunza!" the minute a customer came in. The minute we heard the door-chime jingle.

Oh, you don't know what a runza is? Okay, it's like a Russian calzone. It's yummy meat, ground in with yummy vaguely Russian spices, surrounded by a bun. Thus, the meal in a bunza.

Working at Runza, you were expected to wear a yellow Runza T-shirt and forest-green shorts. Even in winter. Side bar: The owner was a creep. Fun fact: I quit that job by throwing an ice cream cone at him.

You may be interested to know that before the alleged ice

cream throwing, one night in early fall, Zander came strolling in. It was at this point that I dove under the counter, hiding behind the soda machine. So Zander walked into an empty Runza.

"Hello? Heeelloooo, anybody there?" He looked around. And I stayed hidden.

"Um, okay, is anyone here?" And then he continued looking around until he looked behind the counter where I was hiding.

"Daffodil?" This, of course, was before he called me Daffy. Before anything, really. "I didn't know you worked here. Um. What are you doing?"

"I'm . . . um . . . cleaning the . . . bottom of the cabinets." He looked at me then.

"The owner is super strict about cabinet cleansing maintenance."

He gave me a funny look then. "It kind of looked like you were hiding a little bit." He grinned. Somehow shimmering.

"No. I really care about it too! Cabinet cleanliness!"

"Okaaaay." Still shimmering.

"Do you want to order something?" I suddenly remembered I was supposed to work there.

"Actually, not really. Actually . . . I kind of just came here to see you."

Aaaaand my head exploded.

"What? Wait, I thought you just said you didn't know I worked here?"

"I kind of lied." Sheepish grin. "You look pretty cute in your Runza representation outfit."

Oh. MY God.

"I look like a banana."

Shimmer shimmer shimmer.

I really just couldn't take it anymore. "You should probably go. Since you're not ordering anything. See, look, the sign says no loitering."

He looked up at the sign.

"Okay, I'll have a Runza and a shake. Now you can't kick me out."

Gasp.

"I refuse to serve you." I pointed to the other sign. "See. We have the right to refuse service."

"You're a tough case, Daffodil." He smiled and began walking out, casually whistling.

Then just as he reached the door, he turned back. "A very tough case . . . that I intend to crack."

The door-chime slammed behind him as he walked out and the entire Runza, a meal in a bunza, was filled with the air of a shimmering circus.

I remember my stomach taken over by fireflies.

But now here, at the diner, a baby screams and the

moment is broken. I say goodbye to Runza and that twinkling memory.

But, it is true, welcoming customers was part of the job!

My annoyance at being completely ignored overwhelms me and suddenly I am impatient.

No.

No, I won't stay here.

I stand up and make my way to the front door. I throw it open, and the bell tinkles overhead. The customers look up from their mugs, their glowing screens. Waiting.

I want to say something, something clever and possibly withering. But I can't think of anything.

So I leave.

I resolve to make my way to the library.

There I will be allowed to float through the stacks to my heart's content.

There I will speak to no one.

Strolling along the sidewalk of the town, a weed poking through here and there, I notice something in the window of a secondhand store. A random thing, really. A microscope.

A blink—and I'm suddenly back in Biology 101, back with *the* Zander Haaf. Since his sparkling appearance at the Runza, things had been slowly, dreamily progressing. Constant notes, church giggles, a paper flirtation.

And then one day, I'll never forget it, I wrote this:

Stop writing me! Why are you even writing me?

It was kind of infuriating. Everyone knew Zander Haaf was too good for me. Was he teasing me? All this attention—was he just making fun of me after all?

But then Zander replied:

Because I like you.

I died when he wrote that.

But then, my reanimated corpse wrote back:

Why?

And Zander took forever to write:

Because you're strange. And smart. And look kind of like a spooky albino. And in your Runza outfit, you look like a little banana. Oh, and you think weird. You say things weird. Actually, come to think of it, I don't like you.

I looked down. Frowned. O-kaaaaay.

Then, he quickly scribbled:

I'm in love with you.

Ladies and gentleman, *the* Zander Haaf just told me he was in love with me! He wrote it right there! In black and white! For all the world to see!

And my insides went tumbling. There were butterflies dancing ballets. Dragonflies dancing the cha-cha. And the ground ceased to exist. Now I was only floating, floating with my chair and our table in Biology 101.

I didn't reply. Not a note back. Nothing.

I couldn't.

I was paralyzed.

Paralyzed with glee.

Zander, expectant, waited. Waited . . . and waited.

But, you see, I just couldn't. I just didn't know what to do. I was in a state of crisis. Love crisis.

Then, Mr. Eckdahl told us we all had to go to the microscopes and take a piece of our gums, which, gross, how do you even do that? We were supposed to saw off a piece of our gums with a toothpick and take a look at the miracle of our cells!

So, there Zander and I were, trying to saw off our gums and look at them under the microscope. And there I was looking into the microscope, Zander close beside me.

He said, "Do you see the miracle of your cells?"

And I couldn't see them. But I wasn't even thinking about them. Who could care about the miracle of cells when the greatest miracle of all time, Zander Haaf, was standing right beside me, so close I could smell the Tide on his T-shirt.

And then it came out.

Even though I was still staring into the microscope, it came out then and there.

"Zander?" My face buried in the microscope.

"Yes?" he whispered. I could feel his breath on my ear now. Oh God.

"I'm in love with you, too."

I can't believe I said it! And thank God my face was stuck to the microscope because then he was gone.

Gone! He left his spot behind me, and then I was alone at the microscope, and I blew it!

I looked up, confused.

He was sitting back at our table.

He was sitting with his head in his hands.

What?

Oh God. Did he hate me?

Was this whole thing a joke?

Mr. Eckdahl told us to take our seats and I sat back down at our table, next to Zander. Who still had his head in his hands.

"Um . . . I'm . . . sorry?" I said then, not knowing what to do.

His head popped out of his hands. "Sorry?! Oh, no no no *no*."

I'm not sure what the look on my face was at that precise moment. Just imagine utter confusion. However that looks to you.

"Don't you see, Daffodil? Don't you see?" He leaned in and his face was flushed but there was a smile on it. "This changes everything. Everything."

And, again, I was flummoxed. But Zander leaned in, his

eyes on fire. A kind of blue-green fire made of giddy.

"I am going to make you the happiest girl in Nebraska, I swear." Then he paused for a moment, thinking. "You know what, Daffodil? This is the best part. This is the best part of my entire life."

And he looked up at me, then. Even though Mr. Eckdahl was blathering on about cell rejuvenation, and even though it was bright daylight, and even though it wasn't even noon, he spontaneously lunged over and kissed me, right then and there, on the mouth.

In Biology 101!

And he was right.

That was the best part.

Every moment.

Every cell.

Every breath.

Until spring.

Until that night in spring.

CHAPTER 32

I read through almost two entire books in the public library before returning them to the shelves, *A Field Guide to the Yukon Wilderness* and *A History of Scarlett Mills*. The cover of the first book was, you guessed it, a field of wildflowers on a grassy plain, with lots of trees involved. Tips about hiking. What to do when encountering wildlife.

The second had only a cloth binding, sun-bleached blue. The pages were yellowed and fragile. Inside was a collection of overheated legends about the town.

A tale about a creature called the squonk dwelling in the pine forest. It reminded me of stories we used to hear in Nebraska about the Alkali Lake Monster. It strikes when least expected! And curiously a lone member of the party survives to tell the tale.

Seriously? If some *olde tyme* gentlemen wanted to come up with some scary stories to tell *ye olde* kids in the dark? They should have come up with a better monster name than "squonk."

Several stories centered around "the Quince House," which must have once sat somewhere on the outskirts of town. A teacher who bludgeoned his fiancée with a hammer in a jealous rage. A freak fire decades later that killed the house's inhabitants and a worker. The fire was blamed on heat and dry conditions, but the anonymous author of this volume seemed suspicious. Some very hippy-dippy stuff about bad energy trapped. Malevolent spirits.

Creepy.

Normally, I'd laugh.

I ignore the sensation of something crawling along my spine and consider the cover of a paperback volume titled *His Wayward Love*. The cover features a man with a white blouse on, wind-whipped as to show his giant muscles, including a six-pack. In front of him, a woman in a lilac princess dress swooning in his arms. The wind was obviously really whipping up in this picture. I guess that was a picture from before his love goes wayward. Maybe it was supposed to be *His Windward Love*.

I'm very involved in my analysis of that book cover—who posed for it? Did anyone pose for it? Or is it just an illustration? Why is her dress not wind-whipped when his shirt is practically blown off?—when I realize that the sky outside seems to have turned itself from blue to purple. And not a subtle purple . . . the purple of an angry bruise. The kind of sky that, back home, means a tornado.

I turn around, looking back at the town diminishing in the distance. Yes, it's still there. True. But the clouds above it have turned to a deep, aching purple and the air around me is starting to change. The barometer is dropping. This is one of the things you have to know about if you grew up in Tornado Alley. The feeling before a storm.

A storm, where I come from, could mean a light drizzle, or that the entire side of your house gets ripped off, leaving a painting hanging neatly on one wall while the opposite one has been turned into matchsticks of splintered wood with a tractor-trailer cab stuck in the middle of it. So, of the very few things I know, this is one of them: A storm is coming.

I pick up the pace, not wanting to run, although come to think of it . . . why not run? It's not like anybody is watching me. And yet I stick to a merely quickened pace.

Plink.

Plink plink.

The drops come down as mere suggestions at first. As if the sky is saying to itself, "Oh, I might rain . . . still not sure."

Plink.

Plink. plink.

The sky still deciding.

And then . . .

WHOOSH! Sheets of water dropped from the sky.

Okay, now I can run. Now, even if some drone is monitoring me from space, I will not look like an insane person dashing madly down the road. No. There's a reason. It's raining. Hard.

In fact, we've gone way past mere rain now. Now we are at deluge. Cats and dogs.

Normally, this is the moment where you'd duck under something. It would be sweet. You'd huddle under an awning and wait for a break in the storm.

But folks, there ain't nothing here to sidle up to. This is just a field and a dirt road.

The thing about this storm is . . . it's fixing to make some lightning. Again, I know when the sky is about to open up. The hair on your arms stands on end. When the hair on your head stands on end . . . then you're just about to be struck by lightning.

But I'm not sticking around for that part.

It's as if the sky hears my thought, choosing to break

the earth in two as a shot of lightning hits somewhere far behind me, just as I take off from a run to a sprint. Guess I'll be getting my workout today.

"One . . . two . . . three . . . four—"

CRASH.

Okay, that's the thunder.

It's four miles away.

Sprint. Sprint. Sprint sprint.

Heavy breathing now. God, I'm out of shape. I really should exercise more. This is a thought I have: Why am I so lazy? It's only in moments like these that I realize my slovenly ways might one day be the end of me. I mean, suppose I was running for my life, then where would I—

A BURST of light.

"One . . . two . . . three—"

CRASH.

It's getting closer.

That was fast.

What is that expression, a mile a minute? It's actually good that I don't have an umbrella. Or, in this case, you would call it a lightning rod. But even being out in the open is a huge mistake. I'm the tallest thing I can see for miles, and that is not what you want to be in a storm.

It might be time to contemplate lying on the ground and

making myself small. The smallest possible target. If I don't see the house before the next—

FLASH!

"Okay, one . . . two . . . three—"

CRASH.

"Please, God, if you're listening, if you're not too busy, please let me make it back to the house. I promise I'll be good. I promise I'll try not to use your name in vain. I promise not to be mean ever and I'll even pray more and—"

Another flash.

"Shoot. One . . . two—"

CRASH.

"Also, I'll not covet ever. No more coveting! Seriously, God. I'll just never even think about coveting anything!"

Nothing but the sheets of rain to answer me.

But then . . .

There in the distance, I see it. The house, there it is, beyond the bend. A glowing light within.

I can make it!

I can make it, God.

Thank you.

It's the last thought I have before I spill myself onto the front porch just as a bolt of lightning hits the oak tree fifty feet from the house.

CRASH!

It shakes the ground. It shakes me.

In a daze, I can barely hear the sound. . . .

"Come in, come in! Get inside, dear!"

Why is there an English accent talking to me right now? Did I die? Did I go to heaven? Or, worse, hell? I mean . . . an English accent? I always imagined everyone in heaven speaks Italian. Or at least Latin.

A pale hand reaches out to me and before I can process what is happening, I'm smack-dab in the middle of the entry-way, soaking wet, shivering there like a traumatized rat.

Penelope looks down at me.

"Should I put the kettle on?"

CHAPTER 33

"My goodness, listen to that thunder!" But Penelope doesn't have to say it.

There's no way *not* to listen to it.

The entire house shakes after each bolt.

I'm sitting in a wingback chair in the living room, wrapped in a blanket, drinking tea and staring into the fire in the fireplace. Penelope is, apparently, good at lighting fires and keeping the fire aflame. Sounds easy, I know. But it's harder than you think. First, you have to put in the crumpled-up newspaper, then the kindling, then the log . . . then you have to keep sort of tending to it, with the bellows and all these other medieval-looking tools kept next to the fireplace. A wrought-iron menu of fire-tending delights.

But there is something about staring into the fire—it's hypnotic. Something makes you lose yourself in it, lose yourself in thought. Like staring out at the sea.

I don't want to ask Penelope directly why she is even here in the first place, because it's rude. And, quite frankly, I am grateful for her presence. Grateful for the tea. Grateful for the fire. Grateful for the unnecessary exclamations after each lightning strike. But, still, I do kind of want to know. I mean, is she just going to keep on popping up all the time?

And my lucid dream from the other night? The one where sweet Miss Pricklepants turned into a murderous crone? That is right there, lurking in a corner of my mind.

She seems to read my thoughts. "I apologize for intruding, my dear girl. You see, I got swept up in the storm, as well! I was just down the road, there."

Ah.

"Don't worry, dear, I won't make a habit of it." She smiles a knowing, slightly apologetic smile.

Wow. Is this what happens when you get older? Can you just read people's thoughts? If indeed I do grow old, I vow to become a mind reader. I will anticipate everyone's move, every gesture. I will wear funny orange hats with flowers all over them, too.

"I quite like the rain, actually, now that I'm out of it."

She takes the matching wingback and stairs into the fire with me.

"Do you mind if I ask you something, dear child? I can't help but wonder . . ." She trails off.

"Of course."

"Well . . . it's a bit strange, isn't it? A girl your age spending her summer here. In this place? All alone? Aren't you meant to be throwing yourself into the glistening water of a pool somewhere, or frolicking on the beach with friends? Shouldn't you be . . . somewhere else? Somewhere bright and happy?"

She waits for me to answer, sipping her tea.

"Honestly, I don't really have any friends."

It comes out a bit harsher than I planned it.

"Oh." She looks at me. "Oh, I see."

And that's definitely pity I hear in her voice. But the rain outside is pounding the roof, a rhythmic kind of song, and the fire is blazing and it leads my thoughts away.

If I close my eyes and listen to the rain, it sounds just the same as that night. Just the same as that night in April.

April showers bring May flowers. But that's not all they can bring.

If I close my eyes I can see Zander standing there, outside in the rain.

Open your eyes.

Open your eyes, Daffodil.

"Well . . . I'm your friend," Penelope offers. "So, that's set-tled." She pats herself on the knees as if the matter is closed.

"Thanks." It comes out in an embarrassed laugh.

"It's strange how life is, my darling. When I was young, I remember I was surrounded by friends, acquaintances really. Not real friends. But so many I couldn't bother to remember their names. And then, as life goes on . . . they all just kind of drop off. Just sort of get lost somewhere in the ether. And one day, you look around . . . and they're all gone." She thinks. "And one finds themselves wishing they had taken the time. Had kept in touch. Had not spent all that time fussing about this or that, or trying to reach out and grab grab grab this or that. You want to tell them all to come back. To come back to you."

She stares into the fire, a sadness coming over her. And it makes me sad, too, hearing her say this. Or thinking this is the way it is. For everyone. And I hope it's not true. I don't want it to be true.

"Um. So, you know, it doesn't really seem like this rain is going to let up . . . I mean, not anytime soon," I find myself saying.

"Indeed."

She sips her tea.

"You should probably just stay here tonight," I offer.

"Oh, I couldn't." A slight shake of her head.

"No, I mean it. This isn't going anywhere." And, as if to emphasize the fact, a crack of thunder shakes the house.

I smile at her. There's that clairvoyance. See? I'm developing it already.

She contemplates, looking into her tea.

"It's not exactly like I can send you out into the pouring rain to fend for yourself. It's dangerous out there."

I could think about exactly how dangerous it is. I could think about the danger that is everywhere. I could think all the things I'm not supposed to think about.

Or I could stare into the fire and listen to the sound of the rain on the rooftop and politely drink my cup of tea with Penelope Persephone Crisp.

CHAPTER 34

There's nothing strange about this particular night—other than the thunderstorm—until it happens.

Yes, Penelope stays over, in one of the downstairs bedrooms. The nice one. Leave it to her to feel just fine about taking the fancy bedroom.

Perhaps I am too hard on myself.

Perhaps I should tell myself I do deserve the fancy bed.

But I don't.

I most assuredly don't.

There's nothing unusual about bidding her good night, going up the stairs, and brushing my teeth. Nothing unusual about tuning in to *Ancient Aliens*, with the volume on low so as not to be devastated by embarrassment if anyone knew I was watching something so absurd. Nothing unusual about drifting off to sleep with a mind full of ancient artifacts and magical disks.

In fact, there's nothing out of the ordinary whatsoever . . .

Except for the moment I awake with Penelope standing over me.

It must be three or four in the morning, the rain has stopped and in its place is silence, exaggerated by the downpour before it. Perhaps the suddenness of the silence is what caused me to wake. Or perhaps it was the body hovering over me by the bed.

I wake with a start to see, there, just next to me, above me, good old Penelope standing there. Just looking down at me. Blank.

There's nothing menacing about her face, and nothing kind, either. It's a numb sort of thing.

"What the hell?!" I leap to the other side of the bed, dragging the blanket protectively over myself. A shield.

But she stands there still, seeming to shake her head, just slightly. Muttering something to herself.

I lean in to listen. What is she saying? Who the heck is she talking to?

And her head shakes a bit more, the muttering continues . . . mutter mutter mutter, "No, no no no no no."

But she's not even looking at me now. She's turned and is

looking at the bedroom door. She's looking at the bedroom door as if she's talking to someone at the bedroom door. But there's no one there.

"Go away! Go away!" she insists, imploring the air. "Get out of here! Leave her alone!"

"Penelope," I call to her, "wake up. Wake up! You're having a bad dream!" I clap my hands loudly. And then again. "Wake up, Penelope! Wake up!"

With the hand clap she seems to snap out of it.

She looks up at me.

"What are you doing here?" she asks.

"Me? I think the better question is what are *you* doing *here*?" I answer.

She looks around her, befuddled.

"Oh dear . . . Where am I?"

"You're in my room. The attic. This is where I sleep." I'm trying not to sound too annoyed.

"Oh, well, dear girl. What a strange place to choose to sleep. Why do you not sleep in one of the downstairs bedrooms? They're so much more pleasant."

This is hardly the time for criticism.

"I just like it better up here. And, um . . . I'd like to sleep a little more, if you don't mind. . . ."

"Of course, of course. I'm so sorry. So very sorry." And she shuffles out in a state of genuine confusion, her hair a muss and shaking her head ever so slightly.

And I want that to be all.

I really do.

I really want to go back to my dreams about Mesopotamian fertility figures and the Phoenicians in their sleek wooden boats, gliding their gleaming hulls into the Mediterranean, maps of their trade routes in hand.

But there's this thing.

There's this little thing that makes that all go away.

It's that . . .

As she clears the doorway and descends the stairs . . .

I notice something in her hand . . .

Hidden behind the folds of her skirt . . .

A hammer.

And now she turns back to me, perfectly normal, and says, "Dear, I believe you must have misplaced this. I found it right at the foot of your door."

CHAPTER 35

I don't know quite how I get back to sleep after the Penelope-standing-over-my-bed experience, which is, obviously, exacerbated by my horrific murder nightmare about her the other day. But somehow I manage to drift off to dreamland. Up, up, and away into the night sky, where I can see the two lines of the constellation Gemini and the Big Dipper just over there.

Somewhere in between the seeing of these stars, becomes the being of these stars. I am now there, among them, a part of them. As if I am a constellation. All around me I can see the miracles of space, the galaxies, the red giants, the Orion Nebula, and it's a feeling of joy, here, a feeling of floating but being able to direct myself, point myself: This way . . . toward the Saturn eclipse. This way . . . toward the Helix Nebula! And the joy of the flying, the zooming around.

And then a voice, again, a whisper.

"Daffodil, remember . . ."

And at first it's Penelope, but then it changes into *that* voice. That soft, sweet voice that says my name like a gift.

Zander.

"Remember . . ."

I'm looking around now, desperately, looking around trying to find the source of the voice, but it's everywhere and nowhere. It's infinite.

"Zander . . . ?"

But now I'm falling. Falling back down and getting smaller. No power. Just a bleak descent, getting smaller and smaller, shutting in on myself and down down down, toward the blue marble, into the atmosphere, below the clouds, down above the treetops and now through the roof, back into the covers on the bed.

But I don't wake.

I'm still dreaming.

In my dream I want desperately to go back to the constellations, to hear that voice and see the beauty there. To *feel* the beauty there.

But it's impossible.

In my dream now, I hide under the covers, pulling them over me like a shield. Shivering. Scared. Unable to open my eyes.

Begging to wake up.

CHAPTER 36

Dawn, now. The sun coming in.

I'm dreading breakfast. Penelope will be there. But, of course, downstairs in the kitchen, she acts as if everything is super normal. As if last night she did not *come into my room and stand over me with a hammer. A hammer she found at the foot of my door.*

I watch her, sipping her morning coffee as if everything is just peachy.

Finally, I can't take it anymore.

"So, um . . . that was pretty weird last night," I say, hoping to open the matter up for a polite discussion.

"What was?" She keeps sipping.

"Um . . . when you came into my room," I answer.

"Into your room? Don't be ridiculous." She sips, again.

Wait.

What?

"Uh, I don't think I'm being ridiculous . . . I think something really strange happened last night."

She looks at me. "My dear girl. I've no idea what you're talking about."

It's not harsh, the way she says it. Just matter of fact.

"Oh, no no no no. You don't get to pretend that didn't happen. It was insane. And scary. And you don't get to pretend it doesn't exist." I'm trying to keep my temper.

"Scary? What do you mean, scary?" she asks, genuinely curious.

"Okay. Last night . . . don't you remember? You came into my room . . . and you were standing above me . . . with a hammer in your hand," I tell her.

"What an insane accusation!" She looks sincerely baffled.

I'm shaking, trying to contain myself. "I really can't believe you're pretending this didn't happen."

"Dear girl, has it occurred to you that this might have been a dream?" she asks, genuine.

My mouth opens to answer, but then somehow I can't form the words. I contemplate this.

I did have that vivid dream about the constellations and flying. But I'm fairly sure this happened before.

I mean—that this really happened.

"Exactly," she says, taking my silence as affirmation. Case closed! "You were dreaming. Certainly, a macabre kind of dream. But, then again, I don't know you quite that well. Maybe you had a macabre upbringing."

This is a chipper kind of musing about a subject I am finding very unchipper.

"Listen. I don't know what you think happened. I really don't. But I do know that I'm not that comfortable being around you right now," I confess.

"Oh, don't be silly," she deflects. "We've *always* been together."

I stop. *Always* . . .

No. I didn't just imagine it. I know what she said. She said, "We've always been together," and the words send a jolt of fear down my spine.

A *WHOOSH* like I felt that first night when I wandered out onto the grounds.

I feel suddenly sure that I am in the presence of some *thing*.

Some thing that wants to push me out and away. Some thing with a terrible kind of power.

My throat is dry. I force myself to swallow.

"I don't want you here in this house."

"But my dear, you *need* me. You can't flit around through

this place alone. You must remember that—"

I stop my ears, pressing the palms of my hands to either side of my head. *"I don't know who you are or why you're here but I need you to leave right now!"*

The sound of my voice echoes in the room, now silent.

She sighs.

"It's quite alright. I'll just be going then."

She stands up and begins gathering her things.

I look on, feeling a combination of guilt, confusion, and anger.

Normally, I would say something here in the form of an apology. But somehow my mouth can't form the words. I refuse to utter even a syllable that will bring her back. I do not want her back. Ever.

The image of the hammer in her hand.

The image of the knife in her hand.

She grabs her hat, tips it as a final gesture, and says, "Adieu."

I stand there, silent, as she makes her way to the front of the house and then out the front door. I wait a few moments . . . hoping to give her time to leave, to not have to say anything more, before making my way to the front door.

I race to it and throw the bolt.

And there I stand, behind the front door, looking out

the window at her figure making its way down the winding road.

As if through telepathy, she looks back at that very moment.

I stand there, caught.

She gives a small nod, turns back, and keeps going.

I stay behind the front door, watching her saunter down the winding road, until I can no longer see her.

A sigh of relief.

She is gone.

I should feel better, but somehow I feel much, much worse.

CHAPTER 37

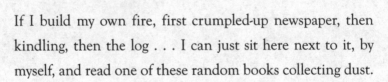

If I build my own fire, first crumpled-up newspaper, then kindling, then the log . . . I can just sit here next to it, by myself, and read one of these random books collecting dust.

So that is what I do. I tend to it like a living thing, getting lost in the flame.

Each flicker takes me back to a random fall day back home. A Saturday. Game day. The ubiquitous sound of football forever on in the background on fall weekends. The sound of home.

Zander's mom was cooking something or other in the Crock-Pot. Something mouthwatering, tantalizing from the smell wafting downstairs into the family room from the kitchen. Every so often she would get up and go stir something new into it. In those moments, Zander and I would sneak a glance. A sly smile. He would kiss me. Every cell in my body would light up. And then she'd come back down the stairs from monitoring the dinner.

And we'd rush back to our PG positions on the sofa.

A giggle in it.

A sweet deception.

And the whole afternoon would go that way.

The Huskers or the Packers on the TV, depending on the day. Saturday or Sunday. Outside, the ground covered in snow three feet deep. An early blizzard that fall, blanketing the earth in white until spring. A winter wonderland delivered early.

And to be in love, in that moment, with those plays and flags and penalties being called in the background, and the smell of some delicious thing in the Crock-Pot . . . was to be on a kind of Midwestern heaven on earth.

And, here, staring into the fire, into the same kind of flames, with all that gone, in this lonely place . . . I could cry that I lost it.

My eyes want to cry, they are welling up, trying very hard to make me human. To give in. To surrender to it.

But I won't do it.

I won't let it happen.

It wasn't my fault.

None of it was my fault.

I swear.

But to go back to it, just for a moment. To rest there, with the whistles and the play clock, with the stew in the kitchen, with the stolen kisses on the sofa . . . I need to rest there, in that time, for just a bit longer.

I close my eyes and imagine it.

My sweetest Zander.

I am with you still.

CHAPTER 38

Monday morning the construction team is back, in all their flannel and denim glory. To take away the silence of this space. To suddenly turn this dirge into a cacophony of activity, nails hammered, boards sawed. Every once in a while, someone yelling over the sound of the drill.

I could see myself, in another time, hating these sounds and these men running rampant all over the place. A proprietary kind of hate. But now, the sound of them calling to each other, the sound of their shovels, the sound of their nails being hammered . . . all of it washes over me like a tonic. They're here. They're back. They exist. This exists. This place exists.

I exist.

I am not just some dream conjured up.

I am a real person.

A live girl!

I don't mind if my *Ancient Aliens* analysis of the mummies being prepared for their space travel is interrupted by a bang here, a drill there. This is all just part of being a human. This is all just part of being a community! Yes. A community of people working in this place together for the same goal. Construction. A guesthouse. Progress.

Not that much progress seems to be happening. Again, with the amount of racket they're making, you'd think they'd have built the Eiffel Tower in the backyard by now. But no, I look back and it still looks like the same hole. A few boards here and there, some string up around the periphery, to mark it. But really, not much. Not to be judgmental. But honestly.

I mean, it seems almost a Sisyphean joke, they hammer and hammer way, and nothing seems to change. They saw and drill and dig. And yet, the same dirt hole.

Obviously, I have no idea what they're doing. So, this is probably just ignorance on my part. I'm sure it's quite technical. A foundation or whatever. Setting the proper structural supports.

I resolve to get back to my beloved *Ancient Aliens*.

Somewhere in the middle of the analysis of the soil

behind the Sphinx, which weather-dating and erosion puts *much* earlier than the pyramids, by the way.

I head down the stairs to the kitchen. The file folder the professor prepared with all the various dos and don'ts of the place sits in the place I tossed it, directly under the window. I gather up the papers to neaten them, exposing the tab on the folder, on which the professor has stuck a laser-printed label.

QUINCE HOUSE.

Strange. Is the professor doing some kind of research project? A new nonfiction Pulitzer contender? Nevertheless, it is thoughtful of him to reuse the folder. Ecologically sound. But of course he probably recycles everything from his coffee cups to his tweed blazers.

Still, it's strange that—

I hear a noise from elsewhere in the house. It appears to be coming from the dining room, which is odd because that is the least active place in the house. It's more of an exhibit. An installation meant to be looked at, rather than actually lived in.

There's a mahogany table and matching fancy chairs, each spread around the table as if waiting for guests to arrive. The walls are filled with oil paintings of very old, very pale men looking down in a decidedly snooty way. Perhaps they do not approve of the menu. Or perhaps they do not approve of the lack thereof. The room is lit by sconces, but they are never turned on because clearly this room is used on extremely rare occasions. A dinner party with colleagues, perhaps.

I imagine the professor and his peers pontificating until all hours of the night while his aloof wife frowns somewhere in the living room before retiring to an early bed.

But there are no academics in there now. Far from it.

Instead, there at the head of the table, as if he's just about to be served the pickings of the feast, is Mike. The boss of the construction crew. His hat is off this time and he frowns down at the table in a pensive manner. Baseball Hat Mike. What is he doing?

"Um, hi," I say, giving him an opportunity to stand up and make an apologetic exit.

Except that's not what he does.

Instead, he sits there at the head of the table, the lord of the manner, turning his head to me in a strange fashion, as if his neck is on a kind of hinge. It's unnatural. Formal. Almost robotic.

"Um . . . is there—"

"I bet the old man has his rich friends over for rich people parties and they all have a good old time right here. Don't you? At our expense." He spits out the words, full of bile.

"Um, well, I mean . . . the professor seems like a really

nice guy, but I don't actually know him so, I don't really know what he does and . . ." I trail off.

He ponders this for a moment. A caricature of thought.

"A really nice guy?" He scoffs. "A. Really. Nice. Guy. Oh, yes, they are all such really nice guys, aren't they? Such really nice guys while they take and take, stealing this way and that way until they have it all and the rest of us just swarm around, begging for scraps!" He bangs the table with his fist.

Oh. My. God.

Okay, so, this guy is clearly having a meltdown right here. Maybe it's the heat?

"Uh, would you like a glass of water?" I offer.

"Would you like a glass of water?" he mimics in the most harrowing high-pitched whine, almost like a puppet of sorts.

Okay, this is getting really bizarre.

"Mike, I think maybe the heat has—"

"Made me crazy!!" He grins a huge grin, delighted by this chance to mock me further. "Oh, yes, I must be crazy. To not accept my place. You want me to STAY. In. My. PLACE!" He stands up, kicking the chair back with the force of it.

He looks at me, a dare. And it's not the force of his movements or his bitter words that are the most frightening here. No. Not at all. It's the wide, insane, teeth-baring grin he keeps plastered on his face. A clown mask of sorts.

I begin backing away.

Whatever is happening here is way beyond my job description.

"Yes. That's right." He speaks now in a softer voice, the eerie grin still glued on. "Seek cover. Seek shelter . . . little princess. Aren't all of you just such little princesses?"

This last part comes out in a singsong.

I stand frozen now. Not wanting to elicit any more words, thoughts, or macabre grins.

He begins walking toward me. "Sweet. Sweet princess. Sweet little girl. The kind of girl you just could never, ever, ever touch or reach or . . ."

And now he's right in front of me. Close enough that I can feel his breath.

". . . defile." He says this last word with an amused smile. "This place!" he bellows. "Everything here is poison!"

Then, immediately, he turns and bounds through the servants' entrance, out the back door, swinging the door out so that it slams in his wake.

SLAM.

I stand there, then bring my hands up and realize they're shaking. Quivering as if I've had a hundred cups of coffee.

My heart, inside my chest, pounding.

I tiptoe to the back door, peeking out, hoping he won't see me. But he is now just with the men, back to barking orders.

I quickly lock the back door.

And then the side door.

And then the front door.

And then all the windows.

And then I double-check all the doors and windows.

A rush of terror in me, catapulting me all around the house. Suddenly, it seems there are so *many* ways to get in. Too many ways. Maybe he could climb up the trellis and open the second-story windows. Oh, yes, that could be. Lock them. Make sure to lock them. Are they locked? Best to check again.

And what about the third-story windows? Well, if it's possible to use the trellis as a sort of ladder, it stands to reason that the third-story windows are barely more difficult than the second. Best to lock them. Are they locked? All of them? Yes, I think so. Best to check again. Best to double-check that check.

And this spasm of activity lasts for the next thirty minutes. A litany of possible entrance points and defenses for each one. I am prepared. I will not let him in.

I check my cell phone. Yes, I must always have the battery charged. Just in case. And, yes, it is spotty service, but there is that landline.

And 911 is just one call away. But, oh God, there is the issue of timing. I mean, how long would it take for anyone to get out here? Ten minutes? Fifteen? Twenty?

A lot can happen in twenty minutes.

I begin searching everywhere in the house for a possible weapon. The kitchen, the pantry, the coat closet.

But then, as if magically appearing, almost a gleam in it. Like there should be a little *BING!* as I see it . . .

There, on the entryway table, right in the middle. I hadn't noticed it before but there it is just right there maybe I didn't see it but how could I not have seen it—

I scoop it up and march up the stairs. Yes, it's a part of me now. Yes, it was there to serve me. Now I have it. It was for me all along. There, in my hand, to protect me. Mine.

The hammer.

There can be good storms and there can be bad storms.

And that's what this was.

Back home.

There was the fun, silly, sweet storm . . . the one where it snowed three feet of snow overnight and the next day school was out. Which is usually a cause for celebration.

Except Zander and I were in love. Crazily in love. The kind of love where it actually hurt to be away from each other, even for a day.

So Zander—foolishly, oh so foolishly!—drove his Jeep over, in the middle of the blizzard, with his older brother, just to see me. Just to spend a moment with me.

And all the adults involved *yelled* at both of us for being so stupid. Scolded us. His mother. My grandmother. They couldn't believe what fools we were.

And we were fools.

Fools for love.

But that is what it feels like when half of you is missing when the other one's away. That's what it feels like to have yearning, a kind of yearning to see someone who you just saw two minutes ago but already you miss them. A kind of love like a dagger.

We were out to breakfast, in winter. Woodees. Christmas decorations all around, draped tinsel. Red, blue, green lights flashing. Rudolph the red-nosed reindeer staring down from above the kitchen. And I asked Zander why he didn't like eggs. I never saw him eat eggs. And do you know what he said? Well, this is what he said: "I don't like eggs because I was eating eggs when my mom came down the stairs to tell me . . . my dad had died."

And I wasn't expecting that, but then he explained, "My dad was a pilot. And that morning his plane had crashed."

I was stunned now, just wanting to hold him gently. To make everything better. To stop time.

And then he thought about it a minute. "Before the eggs, I was just a happy-go-lucky little kid and then, after? Trauma-tized. A little ghost walking around."

Frozen, sitting there, I had had no idea. No one had told me.

Then Zander looked up. "Until you. I've never been this happy before. Since that morning. It's true . . . I just realized it."

And the feeling I had then was . . . gratefulscared? Sadlucky?

"I feel . . . sadlucky," I confessed.

"Daffy." He looked at me. "You're weird."

He smiled then, and I smiled. And he laughed in his smile. "You're so fucking weird." And then we were both laughing. And the diner lady was giving us a dirty look, but what did it matter? What did anything matter with Zander and me, and even though neither of us have dads and only one of us has a mother, none of that matters because we have each other. And each other is warm. And each other is safe.

But that was winter, and that was before spring.

Before April.

When the bad storm happens.

It was an April rainstorm where the sky opened up, but it was a Friday night and when we went to the party there wasn't even a cloud in the sky.

Zander and me.

Over at a party out at a ranch, out in the boonies. Past Highway 2. I didn't know whose house it was but Zander did. A friend from soccer camp.

That friend's parents were out of town.

Of course.

And it was supposed to be a fun night.

A Friday night in spring!

Someone must have thought they were really clever because they spiked the red fruit punch and, next thing you know, everybody was walking around in stumbles, bumping into things, tipsy.

You couldn't taste it.

The punch was in a big plastic bowl, and it was impossible to tell what was happening until it was too late. And by then it was too late for a whole lot of kids. Seniors. Juniors. Even freshmen.

I remember a skinny freshman throwing up in the flower bed outside, right next to the front of the house. His whole body convulsing, trying to expel the poison.

Just before the sky opened up.

And then the poor kid was there, throwing his guts up in the bushes, in the pouring rain. His white T-shirt stuck to his back, hunched over. An awful trick. This poor guy. I felt for him.

And then it got worse. More rain, now in buckets.

All the kids inside, not knowing what to do. Baffled, try-ing to make sense of their weaving feet and water coming down from the sky, water everywhere.

Some people, and there are always these people, were having a good old time with it. Hey, this is crazy! Dancing in the middle of the floor, hands in the air like they just don't care. A DJ keeping the dance floor full, a makeshift dance floor in what appeared to be a family room. A rather large family room, with trophies of deer on the wall, and even a bull head, a giant stone fireplace, and plenty of space to shove the sofas out of the way to make room.

Zander was trying to make the best of it. Standing with me, next to the dance floor, weaving a little, he gestures to the dance floor, now piled with people, arms in the air. He shrugs and leads me to the middle of the dance floor, still tipsy. The two of us, now in the middle of the sea of hands.

Outside, there was a flash of lightning and, soon after, thunder. *BOOM!* The kids on the dance floor shout out, and the lightning and thunder become part of the fun, part of the insanity. Each bolt followed by a wave of hoots and hollers.

And what did it matter if it was storming outside if we were all in there and the party was shaking the animal tro-phies on the wall? What did it matter with all that bass shaking the floor and all of us singing along to the treble? What could go wrong?

No, it was the best night, the fun, silly night, the decadent night, and we were the kids and the kids were alright.

Nothing could hurt us then. Nothing could get in the way. Nothing could make us do anything other than be kids being kids with our arms up in the air and our bodies sweat-soaked and a few kids even had glow-stick necklaces they were putting on everybody. This was how we would do it. This was how it was done.

And now, standing here on the third floor of this cold, dark house, peeking out the window to make sure the workers, all the workers, are good and gone for the night, I would do anything to transport myself back to that time. Back to that moment with the thunder shaking the makeshift dance floor and the hooting and hollering and the bass shaking the walls of the house, the framed pictures barely able to stay put on the walls.

I would go back to that part.

But I would have to be careful, because right there is where the storm went from being a good storm to being a bad one.

CHAPTER 40

It is night again.

I check all the doors and locks. Second, a quick scan of the windows. Third, a thorough investigation of the backyard. This hammer seems to be welded now to the palm of my hand. Letting it go is too dangerous, leaving me too vulnerable.

I am assessing the situation with the flashlight mode of my camera. This wouldn't normally be the best time to do this, considering that it's dark and considerably spookier than during the day. And considering everything is slightly damp.

I understand that.

But, you see, perhaps there is some sort of clue to the

sudden madness of the otherwise boringly normal Mike.

It could be.

The light hits the weeds and trodden grass of the back-yard, shining its spotlight on a screwdriver here, a monkey wrench there. A drill. Terrifying.

What horrible thing could be done with that drill?

I clutch the hammer tighter.

It's not a full moon tonight, not even close. It's a sliver of a moon, keeping the earth dark. Only the occasional *hoo-hoooo* of an owl to break up the silence and the sound of my breath.

The dirt hole they've dug looks pretty much the way it always does. No change. No progress. I tell myself there must be some complicated, logical reason for this. Permits! Isn't that a thing? People are always going on and on about the pain, the hassle, of permits. Yes, that must be what it is.

They have, however, managed to put up a kind of temporary shed back here. A cheap thing bought from Home Depot or the like. It's plastic but painted to look a bit like a red and white little barn.

I can't help wondering what's in it.

I make my way over a few uncut boards, careful with each step not to slice my foot on something grizzly, until I am just outside the fake red barn.

I try the door but it jams.

And then again.

As if something is sticking it closed from the other side. Putting weight on it.

But what could be . . . ?

I look around for something to jack it open with . . . Ah, a crowbar! That will work.

I make my way back over to the plastic barn . . . crowbar in one hand, phone with flashlight on in the other. It's cumbersome and I'm sure I look ridiculous. But I must know!

There again, at the front door of the little barn, I insert the crowbar in the door and begin cracking it open bit by bit.

Bit by bit . . .

There . . .

Almost . . .

WHAM!

The door swings open as if setting itself free.

And I see the thing that was holding the door closed.

Not an abnormal thing.

Not at all.

Honestly, it's just a sack of mulch.

That's it.

"Huh!" I scoff out loud to no one, suddenly realizing how ridiculous I am being.

What was I expecting to find? A scary note? A treasure map? A dead body?

No.

It's ridiculous.

I am being ridiculous.

"Stop it, Daffodil. Just stop." The night seems to be listening to me now. "You're overreacting. Who knows? Maybe Mike just had a bad day. Maybe he just found out his wife has cancer or something. Maybe it was one of those lash-out moments that everybody has every once in a while. A random freak-out."

Hoooo-hoo.

Even the owl is attempting to provide solace.

I shut the fake red barn door and leave the crowbar on the ground, making my way back into the house.

After the minefield of metal things, I am happily through the back door and happily back inside. Then I am happily up the stairs and happily at my room—

And that's when I see it.

CHAPTER *41*

It's as if a trick has been pulled on me. A prank.

There's even a sort of humor in it.

Yes, I can see that.

A sort of irony.

I was here . . . then I went outside to investigate. And then the sinister thing happened back in here. Where I just was. What? A half hour ago?

Not enough time.

Not enough time to do this.

Physically, you see . . . it's impossible.

And yet it is done.

Right here before me.

I close my eyes and look again.

Yes, still there.

You see, how to describe it without sounding ludicrous . . . ? Not easy.

So, what it looks like is this:

It looks like . . .

Someone came into the room.

Took all the furniture . . .

. . . and piled it all . . .

. . . floor to ceiling . . .

. . . like puzzle pieces . . .

. . . upside down . . .

. . . all against the back wall.

!

And when I say piled . . . I mean the furniture is stacked in just a way that you would almost have to have planned it. Like a genius test or a Rubik's Cube or a 3-D puzzle. There is little to no space between the objects, and each balances perfectly, precariously, on top of the other. So that the entire back wall is covered from top to bottom.

I stay there, paralyzed, looking at the thing that cannot be, yet is.

"This can't be happening what is happening how is this happening how is that even possible who the hell did this what kind of sick joke is this" is what I would say if I could utter a word, which I, most assuredly, can't.

I close my eyes again.

Maybe it will go away.

But no.

When I open my eyes, it's just as surreal and inexplicable as before.

I even have the thought, Don't close your eyes again, because if you close your eyes it could change again.

Which is a crazy thought, but why not?

Why not at this point?

If what I'm seeing clearly can't be.

Could never be happening.

Then absolutely anything can happen.

So, I do what anyone in my shoes would have to do at this moment.

I slowly back away, back out to the landing, back down the stairs, all the while staring at the obviously not happening thing, until I am firmly, triumphantly in the professor's bedroom. There, I close the door in front of me.

I notice there's a key in the lock on this side, an old-fashioned silver one. I lock the door without thinking, as I'm in robotic mode now. No room for emotions. And I make my way over to the bed.

I will sleep in the professor's bed tonight.

The professor's bed will somehow protect me.

I get into the bed, pull the covers over my head, and stay there, waiting for sleep to come.

Waiting for some sort of sound.

Hoping not to hear it.

CHAPTER 42

At dawn, the morning light streams through the velvet curtains, awakening me to a posh kind of day. In the throes of sleep, waking up here, you could imagine yourself to be some sort of countess, awakening the day before a ball. A ball! What should I wear to the ball?!

And I wish I could be a contessa right now, with sartorial quandaries and vanities alike. I would stay in the bed all day deciding on my night's adornments.

But as the sun comes in, the circumstances of my not being a countess become evident and I realize what exactly I am. A girl trapped in a remote house where the furniture moves around on its own, where there are scratches on the siding outside, and where everyone around me seems to be going crazy.

Sweet Jesus, can't I just go back to sleep? I will dream about a wealthy, brooding lord who everybody hates but who falls in love with me after many misunderstood signals and prejudiced judgments. He was just surly because he loved me all along! I will dream about the pale blue poofy dress I will wear to the ball with loads of pearls and some giant froofy thing in my hair.

But it's no use.

I am already up and I know what I must do. I grasp the hammer laying on the bed just next to me.

I know my curiosity will get the best of me and before I can complain to myself, I am up and at 'em.

There I go, seeing myself jolt out from under the sheets. There I go, seeing myself pounce up the stairs in one sweeping motion. There I go, seeing myself go to the door and stand purposefully, almost defiantly, in front of it. Waiting to see the impossible thing. As if to say, "Do your best!"

But, of course, there's a new joke now.

A hilarious joke.

Oh, you would love it.

You see, the joke is . . . well, the joke is on me, apparently.

Because the joke is that everything is put back, just so, not a dust bunny out of place.

Everything is just as I left it before going for my night-time constitutional.

I take a deep breath in, trying to slow myself down to ponder this latest insult. Exhale.

Okay.

Okay.

This is the way it's going to be then?

If everything around me seems crazy—is it me who is actually cracking up?

I'm not in good health, brain-wise.

I get that.

I got that, long before I stepped foot in this godforsaken place.

But this is a different level. A level even my exceptional imagination is incapable of conjuring.

No, this isn't me.

This is the *thing*. The one I've felt—so strongly—at least twice now.

"You don't scare me," I tell it.

(It's a lie, of course. But this is exactly the kind of lie that gets you through. A survival lie.)

I taught myself how to lie to myself just like this, last April.

If you learn to do it once, you can use it over and over again.

Down below, the sound of a truck making its way up the winding road to the house breaks the silence.

I know who it is.

Of course, who it is.

And I tell myself a new lie:

It's fine.

I grip the hammer.

Everything will be fine.

CHAPTER 43

That night, back home in April, with the rain pouring down like cats and dogs and the kids on the dance floor as if it were the end of the world. But a happy, crazy end of the world. A glamorous apocalypse!

By this point in the night everyone was starting to saunter off, some to random places where they would pass out—some just seeming to kind of evaporate into thin air.

Whatever happened to them, Zander and I find ourselves the last of a tiny group of stragglers.

"We should probably go," he says.

I remember a strange look, then, as if this was the most absurd idea in the world.

"Zander? Helloooo? We definitely cannot go. How would we even get home?"

The friend, the one throwing the party, stumbled over, patting Zander on the back.

"Dude. You guys can stay. There's tons of room and my folks won't be back until Monday."

Zander sways a little. "Yeah, okay. Sure."

"Cool, dude. No problem!" The friend weaved off to whatever place his bedroom got to be in that sprawling place.

Then I remember Zander turning to me. "We should go."

"Wait, that's the opposite of what you just said. Besides, it's still totally raining and neither one of us can drive right now so—"

He teetered a bit then, as if to emphasize my point.

It doesn't matter, none of it. It doesn't matter to me that Zander is shit-faced because they spiked the punch and he is weaving around and the room is spinning. All that matters is that he is my everything.

"Let's just lie down for a minute. It couldn't hurt. Maybe get some water." All of my suggestions seemed instantly matronly to me.

"Daffodil . . . you're going away next year . . . why are you going away next year?" It came out of nowhere, Zander's voice, coming out in spurts, his thoughts, from brain to mouth.

"What do you mean . . . I'm going away? Everyone's going away. It's college! I don't—"

"Yeah, but you're *really* going away." He stumbled then. "You're gonna go away and never look back. Just. Poof. Burn rubber. You know it. I know it." He frowned to himself, a parody of a drunk person.

"Zander, you're being . . . well, look, someone spiked the punch and—"

"I'm not saying it just 'cause I'm drunk! I mean, I definitely am, but that's not why I'm saying it. I'm saying it because it's true. It's the elephant in the room and you know it."

In vino veritas.

(In wine lies the truth.)

And he was right, yes, he was, right there and then.

I was planning on burning rubber on this place.

Happily. Gleefully. With much joy and abandon.

The only part I wasn't happy about was abandoning him.

I could think about that a bit longer, swirl it around in my mind here in this countessa bed. If there weren't an insistent knock on the door below. Hurling me out of that rainy night in April and back here to this reality, which, honestly is becoming just as strange.

Knock knock knock.

Knock knock knock KNOCK!

I know who it is.

I was expecting this.

It's going to be Mike, the bitter, surly, space-invading Mike. And he is going to want to talk to me.

CHAPTER 44

I know what you're thinking.

Look, I get it.

Why don't I just leave?

But again, you see, there is no choice here. I *can't* leave. I'm strapped. Both metaphysically and financially. Strapped. I have to get through this thing. If I don't get through this thing, I don't get to move on. I know this. I know this so deeply it hums through my veins and sings in my bones.

And, let me tell you, there is no way I'm not moving on. I can't go back home. No way. Not after the thing that cannot be mentioned.

"Hello! Open up! Open up the door here!" His voice echoes off the wooden walls and the moldings.

I contemplate what to do. I'm pretty sure I don't want to open up to someone who already sounds angry. But maybe it's something important. Like the gas being on or the water being off or whatever weird thing has to happen when you're building something.

I make my way to the other side of the back door.

I do not open the door, however.

I just peek out the little window and act polite. "Is everything okay?"

He looks at me, realizing I'm not planning on opening the door.

"Yeah. Yeah. It's okay. Everything's fine." He shrugs, a completely different person from the last time I saw him.

"So . . . what's with the knocking?" I ask.

"Oh, it's just. Well, I wanted to tell you we'd be sawing out back so it could get a little loud." He looks up apologetically.

That's weird. Haven't they been sawing this whole time? No one has given me this warning before.

"Um, okay. Thanks!" I give a quick wave, trying to end the interaction.

"No, but, there was something else . . ." he says. "I was just wondering. There's an issue with the plans I need you to look at."

Is that it? Is there something about being inside the house?

"Um, I'm not really . . . in charge of any of that so . . ."

"Oh, it's just a simple thing. I need to meet with you to show you what I'm talking about. I need you to see the blueprints, because there are going to have to be some slight changes and—" He becomes more emphatic.

"Yeah, um, I wouldn't know—"

"Maybe today's no good. We can just meet tomorrow. After we're done with the work. It will be real quick, just take a minute!" And then he begins walking off, as if it's all settled.

"No, but—" I try to get out of it, but it's too late.

He's already back with the work crew, one of the men scratching his head and looking at the blueprints.

The rest of the day goes by without incident. The noise of the saw does seem particularly loud and unnerving. Around midday, the sound stops.

I wait, then I round the bend and see the backyard has been abandoned, not a worker in sight. And, again, the dirt hole is just as it was. No progress.

I search around for any signs of the schizophrenic boss, but Baseball Hat Mike seems to have disappeared, along with his truck. Good. Then I'm safe.

I let out a sigh of relief as I make my way up the long driveway, up the front steps, and into the house.

My stomach grumbles.

Ramen it is!

I reach under for the boiling pot, my mouth watering even thinking about my soon-to-be ramen feast. I fill the pot and put it on the stove. The water swirls as I watch.

But then there seems to be something else in—

I stagger backward. The pot tips. It spills to the floor.

No, it can't be.

This is not happening this is not happening this is not happening.

It's this place. It's playing tricks. It's tormenting me.

(I deserve the torment.)

The frog from the shelf. The one I saw perpetually swimming in its murky gray jar.

The frog is inside the pot.

My mind races.

I think of the frog from the fable being slowly boiled alive.

The frog who doesn't understand its fate because it can't feel the temperature slowly rising around him.

He doesn't feel it—until it is too late.

Is this a message?

(Is it too late?)

As I stare at the pathetic, maltreated frog, splatted there on the white octagonal tile, I know that I am being watched. I turn, a shiver racing up my spine to the back of my neck.

But there is no one.

Nothing around me for miles.

Yet the feeling persists.

A feeling of something impossible that cannot be happening.

The certainty that that thing is absolutely happening.

I don't know what to do.

I don't know what the hell to do.

No, wait.

I have to get rid of this thing. I have to pick it up and hurl it away and show whatever did this that it is not too late, and I am not afraid.

A shovel. I can get a shovel from the back and scoop this up.

I can dump it in the hole that always stays, the hole that never gets deeper or filled.

Or no, the field!

I look outside.

I will grab the shovel and walk this frog out to the other end of this godforsaken place, and I will leave him.

The owl or any of the other night predators will come along, see the thing, and make a feast of it. All gone.

I will be rid of it.

I march out to the backyard and grab the shovel, bringing it into the kitchen with a clank. I try, without looking, to steer the shovel under the dead frog, again, without looking.

Finally, I succeed. I gently carry the frog in the shovel with the steadiness of a tightrope walker. I walk it gently out the back, over the field, until the house is a tiny doll's house in the distance.

And here I lay it.

Poor, sweet thing.

This is a kind of declaration of war from . . . an unknown source. A sinister source.

The same source who rearranged all the furniture into balancing puzzle pieces on the back wall and then put them back.

A foe.

An unseen foe.

Undetectable.

But malicious.

A kind of malevolent force.

One that takes glee in my terror.

CHAPTER 45

That night, the sky decides to rain again, and I find myself in the professor's fancy bedroom now, trying not to think the unthinkable thought.

But it's no use. The sound of the rain is there, and it reminds me. The raindrops running in rivulets down the windowpane remind me. I look through them, there behind the velvet curtains, and it could almost be like I am looking through the windshield that night.

I begged him not to drive.

I told him we could wait. Just wait out the storm.

But there was something about him that night, some kind of engine driving him to act in ways he had never acted before.

He was unreasonable. Even surly.

And I told him we should stay.

All we would've had to do was stay and none of it would have happened.

"You're leaving so what do you care?!" The words like a whip, lashing out into the night. He threw himself into the Jeep, rain still coming down in buckets. I ran to get in, still trying to convince him.

"Zander. You can't drive. Okay? This is a really bad idea."

"What do you expect you're gonna find there?" He blurts it out.

This stopped me. "What? What do you—"

"What's so great there, Daffy? What's gonna be so great? What's gonna be better than this?" He looks up at me, his ocean eyes and his T-shirt so wet it's stuck to his shoulders. "Better than us. Better than you and me? Do you think you're gonna find that just everywhere?"

I hadn't really thought of it like that.

"Zander, what are you? I can't just stay in this place."

"This place? What's so wrong with it, Daffy? What's so fucking terrible about it? Cause if you ask me, it's pretty good." Then, in a whisper. "The first time I saw you it got good."

The rain still pouring down, ceaseless.

"Right there by the Zipper." He smiles.

"Wait. So you *did* see me then! I always thought you did but I thought I was crazy. I thought there was no way you did." I couldn't believe it. I never thought he saw me that night.

"Are you kidding? I asked every person I could find who that was. Who you were."

"No, you didn't."

"I fucking did. I, like, made a fool of myself. Asking everybody. Who is that slightly albino-looking girl."

"Shut up!"

He laughs. "No, I mean it. I did. And nobody knew. It was so frustrating. I even told my mom about it."

Gasp. "No way."

"Yes way."

"And then that day when I saw you in class, in the doorway of Mr. Eckdahl's class, I freaked out. I couldn't believe it. Cause I found you. It was like the universe brought you back to me. Like it was meant to be . . ." He started shaking his head, upset again.

"Zander—"

"And now you want to leave. You just think that this is, like, normal. Like this comes around every day. And it doesn't. I'm telling you, Daffy. It just doesn't."

"I can't stay here, Zander. It's just— I have a whole life I want to turn into something. I just don't—"

"Just get out."

"That's not fair. What are you—"

"I said get out! Get out and get away from me! You want it over, fine! Make it over!"

"I'm not getting out. You shouldn't drive. You can't drive, Zander."

But then he wasn't even looking at me. Just staring ahead, seething.

And that is when he gunned the engine, hurling us down the dirt road, heading back into town. The roads were muddy then, the wheels of the Jeep spinning this way and that in the mud.

I remember suddenly wishing I had just jumped out. What was I thinking? And then the lightning again, in the distance. The thunder not too far behind. This terrible idea became more terrible by the second.

Remember . . .

KNOCK KNOCK KNOCK!

The rainy windshield now becomes the rainy window of the professor's posh bedroom again. The sound below jolting me back here. To this time.

KNOCK KNOCK!

I look at the clock, an old Victorian thing on the side table.

Midnight. Wasn't it just afternoon? How long have I been here?

Who the hell would be knocking on the door at midnight?

I don't want to know.

I don't want to know anything anymore.

I want out of this place.

KNOCK KNOCK KNOCK!

I try to somehow put myself together, making my way down the stairs to the sound of the knocking, each time, more insistent.

And there in the window . . . he is.

Mike.

Such a plain name. A plain-Jane name.

He lays off the knocking as he sees me, waving a little.

Through the door I hear his muffled voice, trying to be heard over the rain.

"I'm locked out! I'm locked out! Let me in!"

Fat chance.

"I can't get in my truck and I'm locked out! Pleeeeease?!"

A flash of lightning, and I'm in another place altogether.

Or rather, it's this place, but it's broken and burned—a ruin. There's broken glass and the smell of rubber.

A blink and I'm not in the house. I'm on a road.

There is fire and the air is impossible to breathe.

Air like metal.

A crash of thunder and I am back again. Mike at the window. He makes a piteous face.

"Please . . ."

I hear the word and it's another voice. Not Mike's. I hear it and I am drawn to it. I am moving to the door. My brain is crying out for me to stop. To leave Mike to whatever the storm has in store for him.

And yet my hand is on the lock—

and it is turning.

My breath catches as my hand finds the knob.

I open the front door gently.

I let the monster in.

CHAPTER 46

"Oh my God, thank you so much. I had some trouble with my truck there and then I locked myself out, can you believe it? And then this rain, this lousy rain coming down, wouldn't you know it?!"

He tries to clean himself up, excited. "Do you have a towel or something?"

I give a cursory nod and head to the linen closet. From there I can hear him still going on in the entry.

"Can't believe I was so stupid! I mean, of all the dumb, idiotic things to do. And of all the idiotic times to do it!"

I'm coiled like a snake, ready for whatever is to come. I find a navy beach towel and bring it back over to him. He takes it and continues.

"I came back over because I thought I left the plans out. The blueprints. Thought I left them out in the rain!"

"Did you?" I ask.

"No! That's the dumbest part! I left them in the shed out there, you know the shed, that red and white plastic thing?"

I nod.

"Yeah, so I left the dumb plans out in the shed and I didn't even realize it. Then, I come out to get them, not wanting them to get wet in the rain, then I lock my keys in the damn truck! I mean, what the hell is the matter with me?!" He shrugs an exaggerated shrug.

I give him a sympathetic smile.

But something's not right.

He's too emphatic. There's something stagy about this presentation. Something rehearsed.

He's tap-dancing. Around the truth.

I know what that looks like. I've done it six ways to sundown since I was fourteen. Tap-dancing about where I was last night. Tap-dancing about who I was supposed to be with. Tap-dancing about why I didn't get home before midnight.

"But, it doesn't matter now, I guess." He shrugs again.

"Yeah? And why's that?"

"Well, I'm just happy to get to see you." He nods.

"Excuse me?" I freeze.

"Happy to be alone with you. Finally."

There are so many things that I wish could happen right now. I wish that my feet could move backward, but somehow they cannot. I wish my mouth could find the perfect words to end this conversation, but somehow it cannot. I wish I could go back one minute ago, to the time before I opened the door . . . but, of course, I cannot.

"Don't look so stressed. You look so stressed out!" He goes back to being friendly again. A great, big, bright, freckly smile. "You have to learn to relax. Smile. You should smile more, I think."

My throat constricts with fear, making speech impossible.

"Look." He takes a step forward. "No worries. Just think of it like this. We were supposed to have a meeting tomorrow night and now we are having that same meeting tonight. See? No problem," he explains.

There's an energy in his bearing, a slingshot pulled back, ready to snap. I instinctively feel he will lunge.

I try to dissipate that energy.

"I was just thinking. Maybe we could talk about this tomorrow . . . I mean, didn't you say you wanted to show me the blueprints . . . ?" I suggest. "I really want to see the blueprints, and you don't have them right now, so . . . maybe we could—"

"Oh, no. No, no no no no. We are not 'tabling' this for tomorrow. Isn't that the kind of thing you people say? Tabling?" he asks.

You people?

"I don't know. I don't really—"

"Never mind. I don't care." He relaxes a bit, leaning slightly against the wooden doorway. "You know, I just realized, you never told me where you're from."

I stay silent.

"Sooooo . . . missy. Where are you from? Don't be impolite now." He tilts his head.

"I'm from Nebraska."

"Ah! Folks live there?" he asks, casual.

"My grandmother lives there," I answer.

"Ah, no folks then. What happened to your folks? Did you run 'em off?"

I'm silent.

"Now why would a princess like you need to leave Nebraska and come this far to this particular place?" he asks. "Town too small for you? Or is there something else? Something you're running away from?"

His eyes shine like he's in the grip of a fever as he leans in closer. "Daffodil. Have you been a bad girl?"

My heart shatters.

Why is he looking at me like that?

What does he know? How does he know it? How could he possibly—

"It is a strange thing to do. Taking this job, a girl your age, all summer. Strikes me it might get kind of lonely." He pretend-ponders that. "Yeah, I bet it would. Wouldn't it? All alone in this creaky old house. I bet you're just dying of loneliness."

He steps forward and now, like a reflex, I step away. "I think you are a bad girl. Like the rest of us. I think that's why you ended up here. You're punishing yourself, Daffodil. Clear as day. But you don't have to anymore."

"Why not?" I choke out the words.

"Because that's our job." His smile stretches to surreal proportions—a grin so large his mouth stretches from ear to ear, splitting his face in two. Suddenly, everything in the room is out of proportion. Moving somehow. Billowing.

"Poor little Daffodil. It was all supposed to be so different. You were one of the pretty ones. You were headed to your pretty life at your pretty little college." He simmers underneath it. "You were supposed to take that pretty little face and those pretty little blue eyes and those fine words and find yourself a nice wimpy boy from a rich family and live in a house just like this, but in a nicer place, someplace fancy. But it's not pretty to leave the people you love behind. To abandon them."

"That is the last thing I would ever do," I answer.

"That's exactly what you did do, little girl. It was selfish! You are selfish. You play so nice but, ultimately, you're just like everyone else. A cutthroat. You know what it makes me think? Maybe you shouldn't have that pretty little face—the one that looks like daydreams. Maybe you should come with a warning. A face like a warning, ugly as you are inside."

This stops me.

He sees my reaction, laughs.

And now the lock keeping me in place springs open. I lunge toward the phone line in the professor's study.

I pick up the receiver.

No dial tone.

Mike is slow. He sidles up, leaning his head into the study . . .

He smiles. "Now, you didn't really think that was gonna work, did you?"

I put the phone down slowly. Trying to buy time, trying to remember where I put my cell. I could grab it and run into the night.

"Oh, kiddo. Don't even try." He lifts up his hand and dangles my cell, my case, decorated with watermelon slices, and he waves it with glee.

"How did you—"

"You're stuck with me. Here. This is our place. This can be like our little date," he suggests. "Think of it like that."

My brain whirls, and everything goes black.

Do you ever just kind of blank on things that, say, a normal person might remember? Like, for instance, huge chunks of time that seem to have just disappeared into the ether? I have had a few of them. When my mom left. When the-thing-that-cannot-be-said happened. The months that followed. All gone! Just *UP*! Out. Somewhere far away.

And that's how I feel now, staring down at the never-used dining room. Except it's being used now. It's being used by me, who for some reason is wearing a fancy dress. A fancy dress that is not mine and is about two sizes too big.

And I have no memory of how I got here and how Mike is here and how these fancy plates are in front of us. White. With navy around it. With a gold-etched design and gold on the rims. I am staring down at the whole scene from above—like I'm no longer in my body.

"See. Now we get to be rich people." Mike sits across from me, at the head of the table. "It's not just professors anymore!"

The storm continues to rage outside, and in a flash of lightning I see others in the room. They're dressed oddly.

Stiff collars and hats. Gloves on a lady in one corner. An elegant black felt hat, turned to the side, just so. But she is screaming, tortured screaming above the sound of the thunder.

Then silence, abrupt and final.

A crash of lightning and the screams turn into an unearthly screech, the sound of twisting metal, the scrape of steel on concrete.

"Do you not like this? See, I thought . . ." Mike sits back in his chair. Now taking a relaxed tone. "I thought you liked playing games. I thought you liked smiling that little smile of yours and breaking hearts and not taking names. Isn't that the game, yes?"

And now a man stands behind him in a felt cap and jacket. He holds a hammer in his outstretched hand. The man is like the room, billowing. As if cast on some kind of sail. In and out. Here then there. Mike leans in, "You LOVE playing games with people. Do you love this game?"

I can't understand what I'm seeing. Is this a dream? Everything seems more muddled than before, like I'm half in his dream, half in mine. Like I'm slipping in and out of time.

"Do you? Do you like this little game?"

I shake my head, barely.

I'm just trying to keep my eyes on the table. Just keep my eyes on the table, forget about the billowing room.

"Did you steal the frog?" I ask, out of nowhere. I don't even know where it came from, but it just came out in a blurt and then I can't remember if I actually said it.

"What?" He peers at me.

"The frog. You know in the jar?" I look up. "Did you steal it? And then . . . use it . . . to scare me?"

He looks at me for a long moment. He tilts his head.

He walks out of the room, whistling to himself the whole time. The others in the room flash in and out of view, like a TV channel being switched back, then forth. They stand. They disappear. They stare. There's one. Then another. Then another. They lunge for one another. Gnashing their teeth and tearing at each other's clothes. Locked in a kind of undulating battle. First silent, then billowing, then loud as a car crash.

Mike comes walking back into the dining room.

And he has a jar in his hand.

A jar full of murky water.

And in that jar.

Is a frog.

Just like it was the first time I laid eyes on it.

That day with the professor.

The professor.

And then I see him. There, in the room, billowing.

He winks in and out in the space next to Mike, his expression serious as death. Is he trying to warn me? How am I seeing him right now? Why is he blinking in and out? What the hell is happening right now?

Mike very deliberately places the mason jar with the frog in front of me.

It brings everything into sharp focus. Everything into *now*.

The frog doesn't know it's boiling until it is too late.

Silence.

"You're talking about this frog, right? This one right here? In this jar? Right in front of your face," he mocks.

"No, but, you don't understand it was—"

"No-but-you-don't-understand-it-was." He imitates me in a whiny voice. "It was what? It was . . . a figment of your imagination maybe?"

"I'm telling you—"

"You're not telling me anything!" He lurches, and the professor is behind him, making the same movement, his arm swooping down. A double exposure. A mirror world. Mike grabs me by the back of the neck and lifts me up, seemingly through sheer will, with the strength of two men, out of the chair, out of the dining room, and over to the landing, up the steps, and—

The lightning flashes and now the professor is gone.

Now it's just Mike.

"This is gonna be fun. You and I are going to have our date now. You see? It's going to be very romantic. Just like it was supposed to be. Meant to be, my darling." He whispers this last part. "And then we'll be together forever."

CHAPTER 48

We are headed up the stairs now. Mike's grip on my neck like a vise. I can't breathe. I kick my legs, but his hold on me stays firm. A supernatural strength.

On the second part of the landing, there's a side table, which has always been there, except that now there is something on it. Something that wasn't there before.

The hammer.

"You're gonna love our sweet little date," he continues.

The tool gleams silver. Lightning crashes. The lady with the felt hat and full skirt is standing on the landing with us. She picks up the hammer, holds it toward me. She smiles at me, a welcoming smile. She gives me the thought. Yes, this is for you.

Is she real? Is she a dream?

I curl my fingers around the handle.

The cold metal touches my skin.

I feel the weight of it in my palm.

The embrace of it.

"You see, I've always liked sweet little girls like—"

WHAM!

I don't know who did it.

I don't know who did this.

I am looking at him now, his hand clasping his head and his head somehow turning his hand red. His body is weaving now, stumbling back, just like Penelope in that nightmare I had, after the chinoiserie vase crashed into a thousand pieces. And now he lands at the foot of the stairs.

The woman in the felt hat is gone, but as she leaves there are giggles, giggling, and then laughing, and then a cackle. Sinister and ceaseless.

I don't know who did it, but it looks like it happened because of this hammer. And then it looks like it happened because of the hand holding this hammer. And then it looks like it happened because of this arm holding this hammer. And this arm is attached to . . .

Me.

I am the one who struck him in the head with the

hammer in a kind of gesture that seemed like it came from someplace else. Someone else.

"You *bitch*!" He looks at his hand, eyes wide. His entire hand now a deep crimson.

And then he's the one doing something this time. Now it is him on his feet and he lunges toward me, throwing my body backward into the wall of the landing.

My head smacks against the wall. Shapes swirl in my vision, wavering and converging.

And then, again, darkness. Another blank moment. Just like when my mom left and just like after the horrible thing that shall not be named.

And then gray.

Almost like we are suddenly floating in the mist, like on top of some South American mountain in the jungle, a cloud city. The cloud forests of Peru.

And then there's the sound of something.

Like water dripping?

Water being poured?

But it doesn't smell like water.

It smells like . . .

The gas station.

Filling up the tank.

Tank water.

Fire water.

Gasoline.

Someone's pouring gasoline.

Over the parquet floor, over the Persian rugs, over the stairs, just willy-nilly, splashing it around without a care.

With glee.

It sounds like that same someone is laughing.

It sounds like Mike is laughing, but his voice is joined by others, laughing at the same time. Sinister. Mocking. It's several voices joined with a different voice, a deeper voice.

Not even a human voice.

Something much worse.

Something ancient.

And the voice is now laughter, giddy as something sparks.

Whoosh!

A quick flicker and then the spark goes flying and then there are embers. Embers everywhere, flying up.

I'm in the house now. And I'm in the house then. Somewhere the sound of laughter, whistles, and now applause. "Encore! Encore!" And the air ashen and burnt and sharp.

"Encore, maestro. Encore!"

And then the clouds are in my mouth and I'm tasting metal, kerosene, smoke. A spasm. Coughing. My throat, my whole body convulsing, turning itself inside out to get out of these ash clouds.

There are so many figures now, and they're dancing—at the party back in Nebraska, and in the library in Scarlett Mills. The figures dancing and hooting and hollering. The flames are gathering and rousing each other and raising, reaching their fingers to the roof.

And now suddenly I'm in the Jeep.

And the not-think-about box is open.

I'm thinking the things I never wanted to remember again.

It is that night. In April.

This was the night of the party.

When Zander who shouldn't be driving was driving, and when the Jeep, the Jeep that shouldn't be on the road was swerving, and when the rain was falling in buckets, and then the road curved, and then we were spinning. Careening. Suspended. Across the double line and SMASH in the ditch, with the flames rushing up out of the engine.

And I was trying. What was I trying? I was trying to get Zander to get up. Get up get up get up! And I was yelling at him. I was hitting him but he wasn't moving. Why is he not moving why is he not moving?

But how could he move with this face like that? How could he move with his face pinned against the wheel like that? How could he move when the steering wheel was keeping him down and his eyes were open and somehow he wasn't seeing me or hearing me. His eyes were open but they were glass eyes. They were deer eyes. They were trophy eyes. Just like on that wall at the party. Now his eyes were trophy eyes. But not the kind anyone would accept.

And the fire was burning my face, getting closer. I barely squirmed out of my seat, panicking, and I thrust myself out of the burning-up Jeep. And I left. I left him behind. Zander, just like he said I would, just like he was crying that I would as he tore down the road. I was rushing as fast as I could, and all I could think was, this is my fault. I did this. I made him love me and what did I plan to do with his love but leave it behind? In the dirt. In a ditch by the side of the road.

And that's why I can't remember.

Don't you see?

That is why I can't remember any of those things that happened after that. The cars and the lights, swirling blue and red, the red of the ambulance, the red on everything, over everything, and then the blue of the lights. And that is why I can't remember the hospital or the kind words or the candles and the flowers and the pats on the back and the packing of clothes and the taking of trains to get to this place and, this place, this place of a cloud city turning to exhaust.

Because without me, none of this happens. Without me, Zander is alive.

I am the reason Zander Haaf is dead.

My body in spasms now, back in this place.

Back in the fire.

My body trying to throw up this air, but the air coming back in, somehow more vicious in its attempt. The taste of smoke, of chemicals.

And I think I see something, although I can't be seeing it. Yes there, at the head of the table. Mike is sitting like he's still playing rich. Except these flames have come to the party, reaching their tendrils into the air, snaking their way up, and they are enclosing him, enveloping him. Devouring him. His face, a circus smile, wide and to the ends of his ears. From ear to ear, a horrible big-top grin. And the flames love his grin, too, they are loving his grin so much and his smile so much they are devouring him whole and biting him biting him eating him up.

And the smile stays on his face, plastered there, even as his body slips forward.

Even as his body slips forward and bangs on the now burning table and falls to the floor, sideways. A zombie corpse. Smiling even then, from the floor. Happy to be sideways on the floor. A happy face mask.

And I see that mask, I think this is what I get. This is what I deserve. To die here, in this place. But at the same time another voice tells me, "Get up, Daffy. You don't belong here. Get up." My arms decide and my legs hatch a plan to move my body across the floor, drag my body from the landing, still low, over the floorboards, still low, out of the dining room, still low. And I see that grin, still, as my arms and legs decide to take my body out through the kitchen, over the tile, and out past the cupboards and the nook and out into the backyard, elbows and knees giving up as I lay there, outside, breathing the air, the cloud city turning to flames and the house looking down at me, a wildfire in stone, malevolent, seething, looking down at me as if to say, *We had you.*

No, I think as my lungs fill with air. *No, you can't have me.*

CHAPTER 49

The Bryn Mawr library isn't actually in the same architectural style as the rest of the campus. Gothic. Stone. They say it was modeled after Oxford, but it's more helpful to think of it as Hogwarts. It's basically the Hogwarts campus. I'm sure there are a few budding wizards here. Maybe even I will turn into a budding wizard in this new place.

But the library was built in the sixties and is a kind of tribute to bleakness in the modernist style. Oh, let's face it, it's ugly.

There's an uber-modern science library built in the nineties that at least makes an attempt toward beauty. There is, also, a Gothic library, which is actually an extension of Thomas Great Hall, a beautiful gray stone building in the

Gothic tradition. So, that's more of the Harry Potter thing. You could definitely find Hermione in there, laser focused on her burgundy-bound book of spells and potions.

But this library, here, this main one is the hideous one just off the green, where I am gathering all my books for the fall semester.

My freshman year at college!

Can you believe it?

I know. I know what you are wondering and don't think for a second I don't.

You think I skipped.

But I didn't skip. I'm getting to that.

The librarian at the front desk looks exactly like a librarian except that the tips of her hair are blue. Deep blue. Very chic.

It's all a subtle kind of chicness here. No one is going all and all out to get their freak on. It's more of an underplayed rebellion against the patriarchy. A pixie cut. Bangs. Purple hair. And definitely, never, perish the thought, definitely never ever any makeup.

Also, they seem to be spelling the word "woman" with a Y around here. Like "womyn." I haven't tried it yet but who knows. When in Rome.

I've been trying to piece together the moments since the entire house was set on fire in a fit of insane glee, to the moment of actually making it here to Bryn Mawr, collecting my things, finding my room, sauntering to the library.

There is one thing, very distinct.

The lady in the hat coming back. Penelope. Miss Penelope Persephone Crisp. I remember clearly, her voice. That royal pronunciation British accent and the soothing sound of her voice, a different kind of pitch for her. That is seared in my brain.

"I came as soon as I heard, my dear, girl. What a fright!"

I remember smiling to see her, feeling a kind of bliss just at her presence. A relief. Some kind of mother figure here to make it better. Here to make it all go away.

"Don't you worry, dear. We'll get this all sorted." She patted my hand gently.

"Now rest, dear. We've many things to do. But fear not. I am here. Penelope is here. We are in this thing together, mind you. You'll always have me."

I can't help smiling to myself when I think of it. How lucky I was to have met her. How much she has meant to me. How she soothed me. And, yes, a pang of guilt, too. For having sent her away.

And then it's blank again. My memory—a long blank nothing.

But it's no matter. Because now I'm here.

A very studious-looking woman scurries past me in wiry

glasses, hunched over her textbooks. There must be at least four thick volumes, and I can't decide if she's bent over from the weight of the books or simply from being in a state of hyper-focused thought. I understand the feeling. See, I am with my people now!

Anyway, she hurries past me without a glance and somehow this fills me with glee. Others completely lost in thought! What a joy! What a wonder!

The sun is beginning to lower itself in the sky and I begin to panic about the coming week. Classes start tomorrow and I have so much to do. I can't decide between the Ancient Babylonians or "The Poetics and Politics of the Sublime," which is the actual name of the course, don't make fun.

There's a funny little section of the library meant for kids, although I can't imagine why it's here, other than perhaps for the children of the professors. It's only a nook so clearly it's almost an afterthought. But a cute afterthought. An afterthought of color.

There are little furry seats here and little tables. A few stuffed animals and some multicolored kites harnessed above, five of them, flying above, forming a kind of rainbow skyscape.

There's something charming and reassuring about this place. As if it's a second chance at a beautiful childhood. The childhood we all want. The childhood so few of us get.

I take a seat in one of the little furry chairs, a bright blue one. It's a bit small for me but not too bad. I'm little. Always have been, always will be. I don't get to be one of those girls you see with long arms and legs, strolling down the runway like she's about to kill everybody.

The outside light comes through the modernist steel-framed windows, painting this children's nook in a pinkish orange. Coral. Bright and gleaming.

And there is hope in it. Hope in this place.

Kindness.

I'm practically giddy thinking of all the friends I will have here. All the friends I will make. Nervous, strange girls, just like me. Girls who live in their heads like the rest of the world seems to live in their wallets.

I imagine myself laughing, or trying to keep from giggling in class, at some of the boys from Haverford or Swarthmore who've decided to take a class at Bryn Mawr, thinking they could be "with a lot of chicks." We would eviscerate them with a word. We will be in it together. We young women. We will make ourselves safe. Safety in numbers.

They won't be able to touch us here.

And isn't that why we came here?

To be safe?

I'm just about to make my way out of the library, back to my dorm, Radnor, and up to my tiny room on the fourth floor. Apparently, the rooms get better as each year passes, with rooms looking out on the green, with actual stone fireplaces, reserved for a few lucky seniors. These are the many happy facts I remember jotting down in my interview, what was that . . . a year ago. A happy year ago, before the— No, don't think about that. How can you think about that at a time like this? We are here. You made it!

But before I exit the little nook, I see something. Out the corner of my eye I see something and I want to not see it but I see it. And I don't believe I see it but I see it anyway.

Even though this is the children's nook, there are a few beloved books here I can remember. *The Lion, the Witch and the Wardrobe*. *The Lord of the Rings*, Percy Jackson, and, of course, Harry Potter. There are all the Dr. Seuss books from *What Was I Scared Of?* to *The Sneetches* to *The Cat in the Hat*. But there is one book here. One book. That stands out among all others.

You see, this is a book I read, or was read to me, actually, when I was about four. Before my mom left. It was the last book, now, come to think of it, that she ever read to me. It was a silly little book, not that famous, and I had completely forgotten it. Until now.

Maybe, like all bad things, I had put it into the basket of bad things I didn't think about and left it there for good.

Until now.

But, it's really too bad I had put it in that particular basket because if I hadn't put it there then I would have remembered the name: *The Persnickety Patron of Pemberly Place.*

And, also, if I had remembered it, I would have remembered the cover. Which features none other than said Persnickety Patron in front of her dear Pemberly Place.

And, if I had remembered that, and remembered that cover, I would have remembered that this Persnickety Patron looked exactly, not one millimeter different, from Penelope Persephone Crisp.

But how?

My knees start to buckle a little and the wall is now my crutch as I pick up the book, stare at the cover, and puzzle over it.

How on earth can Penelope be on this cover? I mean, this makes no sense. This is entirely fiction! Isn't it?

I look to the back cover, a serious-looking woman with short red hair and glasses. I read her bio. No, it's not true! Of course it's not true.

What, are you surprised when I tell you that *The Persnickety Patron of Pemberly Place* isn't a true story?

No, so this is an entirely made-up character.

One that comes from the last book my absentee mother ever read to me.

And this is also who I've been speaking to all summer.

Hanging out with, drinking tea, building a fire.

I slide down the wall, ending up in a kind of depleted crouching position as I realize, impossibly . . .

I made her up.

I made up Penelope Persephone Crisp.

She is a 100 percent, bona fide, completely made-up illusion from the pages of a childhood book, that I thought with every fiber of my being, was real. In real life.

I made up a person.

I made up a person who maybe was a part of me all along.

I thumb through the first few pages of the book and, yes, there it is! Clear as day.

Penelope Persephone Crisp.

That is the name of her character.

In this book.

This made-up book that I made up into real life.

And then, the dreaded thought hits me.

Wait a minute.

If I made her up, then what else did I make up?

I barrel my way toward the study area with seven rather dated computers, waiting to be lit up.

The professor. The professor. The professor.

What was his name? What was his last name? I struggle to see it in my head, white rectangle sticker on the *New Yorker* subscription . . . B. Q . . . Barney. No Barnstable.

No . . . Barnaby. Q something. Quince. Barnaby Quince!

I type the name into Google faster than I thought possible, and there it is. The very first link:

Scarlett Mills Gazette, August 13, 1865
The honorable Dr. Barnaby Quince and his wife, Mary
Elizabeth, have perished in the house fire of 221 Stanton
Hope Lane on the night of August the third. The cause
of the fire is unknown, but may be due to construction
currently underway at the home. Building materials, paired
with the high summer temperatures and low precipitation
of the season, may have caused the combustion that
sparked the deadly blaze. Services for the doctor and his
wife will be held at the Holy Trinity Lutheran Church,
Sunday, August 15, 1865, in the year of our Lord.

Deadly blaze.

The professor?

My head is in my hands now. I don't want to make a scene.

A pair of giggling girls walks right past me and I try to compose myself, not wanting to establish myself as the freshman freak before classes even begin.

But they don't even glance at me.

Not a nod.

Nor a polite smile.

Wait.

What?

What is happening here?

I leap to my feet and run out of the library, down to the green. I walk across the green, looking at everyone walking by. Everyone. Just walking by. Just chatting away. Ten, fifteen, twenty people.

All chatting away, chirping happily.

And none of them see me.

And again, I hear the voice. That voice inside my head like a memory.

"Remember . . ."

CHAPTER 50

This is like that moment in a movie when everything gets distorted and all you see is the lead actor's face and the rest of the world goes fuzzy in the margins.

This is like that moment, with me waving my arms, and yelling, and jumping up and down, and getting into everyone's line of vision and nothing.

Nothing.

I have an invisibility shield.

A cloak!

And now it all makes sense, as I make my way through the students and professors and some tearful parents sending their kids off to college for the first time. None of them see me.

Now it all makes sense as I take a seat on this stone bench at the end of the row of trees and continue to watch as the people go by, not seeing me.

Now it all makes sense how I don't really remember anything past the point where the blue and red sirens went around in swirls and the red red ambulance and the red red blood was covering Zander and covering the steering wheel and covering the dash.

Now it all makes sense how I don't remember anything after that point in the April rainstorm, the crash, or the kind words from my grandma, or even my graduation, or even the fuzzy details of the trip here on the train. The tickets. The money. The conductor. None of it remembered—

—because none of it ever happened.

And now it all makes sense how none of the waitresses in town ever saw me, that the librarian never noticed me, just let me walk the stacks all day—that none of the people in town ever stopped me.

I can't remember even one interaction with anyone in the entire town.

It hits me.

A jolt.

I never left that red mangle of steel in the ditch.

CHAPTER *51*

When the thought comes to my head, there's a panic in it. A feeling that I'm supposed to be doing something but I don't know what it is but I'm supposed to be doing it.

A promise unkept.

But then, something happens to the green grass laid out in front of me, an emerald carpet.

A lightness to it.

A feeling, somehow, of a secret garden.

A glimmering green garden.

The campus green, the row of trees, seems to have taken on a new life, somehow sparkling. The elms, with their bright green leaves bending over this grass promenade, a canopy from each side, seeming to shutter like a magic spell in the wind.

The cherry blossom trees, farther up toward the library, an impossible shade of pink. A candy pink. A bubblegum lollipop.

And now somehow, even though all these scurrying, pensive students are skittering past me, not noticing me, not a one, there's no panic to it. Not anymore.

It's done.

The thing is set.

Let be.

And somehow there's no terror in it, in all that I thought not being and all that I didn't think actually being.

I had it twisted.

I got it wrong.

But that's okay.

Everything is okay.

And I'm walking through the grass and everything is light, suddenly, peaceful.

Everything is as it should be.

And there is one student who seems to see me.

Coming down the long promenade. Through the canopy of leaves overhead, a million shades of green with some lilac blossoms thrown in.

He is headed right toward me.

Coming closer now.

A kind of calm washing over me. And then, I can just make him out. I can just make him out but he's still so far away. So far away but somehow closer, somehow brighter, somehow shinier.

And I gasp to see.

To see who it is.

To feel who it is in every millimeter of my body.

It's . . . Zander.

My Zander.

Who I haven't seen since the night of the rain in April and the Jeep and the crash and the mangled steel and the blue and red lights swirling, swirling in the night sky.

I have never thought of this moment because I believed this moment does not exist. Could not exist. Never would exist.

Without me saying it, he looks straight through me and gives me a nod. As if he read my thoughts:

Yes, it exists.

Daffy, you weirdo.

There are a thousand questions I want to ask, but somehow he puts this thought in my head. Right smack-dab in the middle of my brain, between my ears:

"I've been waiting for you." A twinkle in it.

"What? How can you have been waiting for me, how could any of this—" I interrupt.

But he calms me.

"You were lost." He finally reaches me across the green. Standing before me, he gently moves my chin up with his finger. "Did you hear me calling you? You needed to remember before you could come."

And now it comes to me. The dream in the constellation. The voice in whispers.

And I notice now that he's not a person. Or not a person how you normally think of a person. He's sort of . . . there and not there. He's sort of shimmering. His eyes are sort of every color green and every color blue and every color silver. They are the perfect color. And they are alive.

"But where was I? What was that . . . place?" I ask, thinking about the stone house and the made-up everything and the fire.

He shrugs. "Someplace that you weren't supposed to be. Someplace you put yourself. But you never needed to, Daff. You never should have. Understand?" He nods.

"Supposed to— But what was it?"

"It's a place . . . where you knocked on the door . . . and they invited you in. But it was a bad place. You were never supposed to be there."

"But did it exist? Is it still—"

"Daffy." He laughs. I love him calling me Daffy. "Do you really think any of that matters now?"

A glittering in his eye. A thought not said, but conveyed somehow: *There is so much to learn, so much I can't wait to show you. You and I. I found you.*

And the thing, like a blast through every cell, unsaid, but still like a shock wave: A kind of giant love. World-overpowering love.

That moment at the Zipper, that moment at the microscope, that moment with the football game in the background, and the Crock-Pot, and the stolen kisses, and the blanket of snow on the ground. All those bright moments, big bright shining moments, all here now.

All in this moment.

Here.

The green canopy above seems to be surrounding only us now. As if the Earth, now, has sent itself to sleep.

"And now it's time," he says, soft.

"Time?" I ask. Maybe I'm just dreaming this.

"Time to come home." He reaches out his hand, gently, and now there is nothing around us. Not even the grass below our feet. Not even the ground. "Have faith, Daffodil."

The sunset light painting everything in gold. Gold, pink, lilac, rose, gold again. A master brush. A virtuoso stroke.

And this is the part I can't tell you.

This part . . . this place . . . the beginning of this place.

If I could, if it were allowed. If I could, if there were even words to tell it. Oh, I would dazzle you with it.

They would be words made of diamonds, new words made of sapphires and rubies and pearls. They would be words made of emeralds. Words made of Christmas. Words made of sunlight. But there are not these words. For you. Not yet.

But if I could, I would tell you how, just how, it is light and it is shimmering and it is all the colors, every color, new colors, and it is so . . .

so beautiful.

ACKNOWLEDGMENTS

I am so grateful to my editor, Kristen Pettit, for elevating the work, always, and everyone over at Harper. I would like to thank my mother, as well as the rest of my family, for the love every step along the way. I'd like to thank my best friends Brad Kluck, Dawn Cody, Io Perry, and Mira Crisp. And finally, with all my heart, I'd like to thank my husband, who is understanding of each step of the process and of my particular case, in general. I tend to be a slightly strange person to actually live with, and my husband embraces my generally bizarre behavior. And, last, but not least, my little boy, Wyatt, who is so effervescent, curious, goofy, and witty, that every day is a new adventure, not only out into the world, but into my own being. How infinite the heart is! It's all for you, Wyatt, my little prince.

Read on for an excerpt from

one

Pedaling fast fast fast, this is the moment. One of those movie moments you never think is gonna happen to you, but then it happens to you, and now it's here.

Pedaling fast fast fast, this is my only chance to stop it. This is the place where it looks like everything is gonna go horribly wrong and there's no hope, but then because it's a movie there is hope after all and there is a surprise that changes everything and everyone breathes a sigh of relief and everybody gets to go home and feel good about themselves and maybe fall asleep in the car.

Pedaling fast fast fast, this is the moment, this is the moment I get to remember for the rest of my nights and my days and my looking at the ceiling. Over that hill and down the next, through those trees and past the school.

Pedaling fast fast fast, this is the moment, by the time I get there you can see the lights going blue, red, white, blue, red, white, blue, red, white, little circles diced up in sirens and you think you can stop it but of course you can't, how could you ever think you could?

Pedaling fast fast fast, this is the moment.

This is the moment, and it's too late.

two

You're never gonna believe what happened. Okay. Let's just start from the beginning.

Logan McDonough's dad bought him a moped. That was the first thing.

Let's say Logan had showed up first thing, first day of school, tenth grade, at Pound High School, Lincoln, Nebraska, having never ever set foot here before, on his black moped, in his black mod outfit, with his black mod haircut. He woulda been a hit. Even Becky Vilhauer, aka number one most popular girl in the school, aka Darth Vader, woulda swooned.

But he had been here before, in ninth grade. When he was a nerd.

So you can see how his actions were totally illegal.

You can't just decide somewhere between May and August that you are going to change your whole identity, jump from geek to cool kid, get a jet-black haircut, peg your jet-black jeans, lose twenty pounds, and drive a Vespa. No way. That is totally against the rules and everybody knows it.

The audacity! Becky Vilhauer was not having it. I know, because she was right there next to me when he pulled up to school and you shoulda seen her jaw drop. She was *pissed.*

If you're wondering what I was doing standing right there next to Becky, aka the dark side of the force, it's because I am number three in the pecking order around here. I have no hope for rising above my station and I will explain why later. But number three is where I will always be and, as I am constantly reminded, I am lucky to be here.

Between number one and number three is Shelli Schroeder. Number two. She's my best friend even though she's kind of a slut. She told me something I immediately wanted to unhear and now I'm gonna tell you and you too will immediately want to unhear it. She makes out and even does the old in-and-out with the high school rockers. Like a lot. One time she told me Rusty Beck told her she has "the biggest pussy he's ever fucked." Yup. Try to unhear that. Nosiree, you cannot. By the way, she told me this like it was a compliment. I didn't have the heart to tell her I'm pretty sure that wasn't going to get her a date to the prom.

I like Shelli but it's kinda weird how she draws on her eyeliner. She kind of just circles both her eyes so you just get these two black almonds staring at you all the time. Imploringly. There's definitely something about Shelli's look that makes you feel like you're always supposed to help her out in some way. I guess that's why those rocker guys are always helping her out of her clothes.

Okay, so the reason why I'm number three and can never even hope to dream of being number two or number one is because my dad is Romanian and looks like Count Chocula. Seriously. He looks like a vampire. Never mind that we never see him and that he lives half the time in Princeton and half the time in Romania. That doesn't matter. All that matters is that he left me with a weird last name: Dragomir. And, to seal the deal, an even weirder first name: Anika.

Anika Dragomir.

So, you see, there is no hope.

You try going to a school of Jennys and Sherris and Julies with a name like Anika Dragomir.

Go ahead. I dare you.

But right now, that's not the story. Right now, no one can believe how Logan drives up to the front school steps.

Like a total. Baller.

And even better, he doesn't even acknowledge Becky

Vilhauer when she scoffs at him on his new moped.

"So, what? Now he's a nerd on wheels?"

And this is what's so weird about the whole thing: Even Shelli notices, which she tells me later on our endless, seriously endless, like we-should-be-put-in-child-protective-services endless, walk home from school. Logan doesn't notice what Becky says because he's not even looking at Becky. And he's not looking at Shelli, either. No, no.

Logan McDonough—nerd-ball turned goth-romance hero—is looking directly, and only, at *me*.

three

By the time I get home my stupid sisters are already locked in their room listening to the Stones and talking on the phone to more boys who don't like them. My brothers are in the back, probably setting fire to themselves or killing something.

In case you're wondering about the pecking order around here, it goes like this: My oldest sister, Lizzie, the leader of the pack, is the one who looks, dresses, and acts like Joan Jett and teases me endlessly for having boobs 'cause she is flat as a board, so fuck her. The second oldest is Neener, she kinda looks like Bambi and as far as I can tell her only distinguishing quality is she likes strawberries. Next up is Robby, he's the happy-go-lucky one everybody likes and never has any problems and looks all bright eyed and cute, like the Gerber baby. Then there's my other brother, Henry, who looks like Peter Brady and has been brooding ever since he was three. And then, last but not least, there's me. I'm the youngest and the one that everyone has decided is mentally deranged.

They're wrong, of course, but I don't mind letting them think that, because everyone lives in constant fear I'm going to kill myself and that's alright with me.

I bet you think I have dark hair and dark eyes and look like I listen to the Cure but you're wrong. On the outside I look like vanilla pudding so nobody knows that on the inside I am spider soup.

Unless they look closer.

For instance . . . Yes, there is blonde hair, blue eyes, pale skin. That is true. But, you see . . . everybody around here has a button nose and I have more of a nose that looks like it got lopped off by a meat cleaver. There's another thing, too—I have a boy jaw, like a square jaw, and cheekbones you could cut yourself on. Also, there are dark purple circles around my eyes that might be adorable if I was a raccoon. So, you see, I'm hideous. Also, there is the fact that Becky constantly calls me "immigrant." That doesn't exactly help.

And yet . . . If you don't look close enough, you would never know I'm not made of apple pie. You have to truly inspect me to see that I am obviously from a place where

Vlad the Impaler is everybody's great-great-grandfather and you have to survive on one turnip a week, which you have split with your brothers and three cousins who live in the attic.

But this is not a complete liability. In fact, it's probably why, two years back, I won that fight at the roller-skating rink. Here's what happened: Russ Kluck, from the wrong side of the tracks, liked me and kept trying to get me to couples skate with him. Even though everyone knows he lives in a trailer, everyone thought I should be flattered, but I don't really know how to talk to boys so I just sprayed ketchup all over him.

He thought that was cute and liked me even more but that just made this other wrong-side-of-the-tracks girl jealous. She liked Russ and couldn't believe I sprayed him with ketchup. I bet she thought she was getting into a fight with a vanilla wafer on roller skates but little did she know she was getting in a fight with a spider sandwich.

Look, I'm gonna explain my insect insides but you have to promise not to feel sorry for me, okay? This is not a sob story. These are just the facts. Plain and simple.

My dad, Count Chocula, basically kidnapped us and brought us with him to a castle in Romania when I was three. Maybe it was more like a chateau. Whatever, to a three-year-old, it felt like a castle. It was me, my real sister,

Lizzie, and my real brother, Henry, practically all alone in that castle, with Count Chocula gone half the time but that was okay because when he actually was there it was kind of like having a walking wraith eating your Cheerios with you. I'm serious, this guy could basically freeze the air just by strolling in the room. It's not like we ever did anything wrong, either. Are you kidding? We were too scared. It was obvious if we even spilled a drop of milk on the stone castle floor we would be encased in glass and sent into the phantom zone, never to return. Luckily, there was a nice nanny for a while. But he got her pregnant and she left.

My mom didn't have any way to get us back so it took me standing up to my dad when I was ten to finally get back home to her and her new husband. So, to recap, I was raised from three to ten by a wraithlike vampire in a freezing stone castle in Romania. Don't feel sorry for me, that's not what this is about. This is about spider stew.

Wrong-side-of-the-tracks girl didn't know what she was going up against at the roller-skating rink and I don't blame her. The legend goes that I pulled her hair out, dropped her to the ground, and kicked her repeatedly with my roller skate. But that's not what happened. It was more of a weird roller-skating dance—each of us pulling on each other and moving in a slow, deformed circle—that was ended by the manager. In all honesty, it was a draw. I guess that girl had a pretty tough rep, though, because nobody ever messed with me after that.

My sisters and brothers don't mess with me either, but that's because not only do they think I'm annoying and hate bringing me anywhere, but they are also worried I'm going to throw myself off the nearest bridge on their watch, in which case, they will be grounded for life.

Robby and Neener, my stepbrother and stepsister, are 100 percent purebred all-American. Their mom lives in a trailer next to a lake and there's even a horse. Also, a duck. Or so I'm told. They have no idea how lucky they are. I would give anything to have a dad who lived in a trailer instead of a castle, and maybe that sounds completely backward but you try growing up half vampire in Nebraska.

Henry, my real brother, doesn't care about being a half-breed because he knows once he graduates from Harvard and starts making a billion dollars no one will care and he can just buy all his friends at the friends store. And Lizzie. Well, Lizzie has decided to just go straight past half-breed, and full speed ahead into super-freak. She is dark. She is gamine. She is mean. She is Joan Jett. She will kill you. And you will know her by the trail of dead.

So, really, I'm the only one around here wrestling with an immigrant complex.

I bet you think I go to school with all these freaks but

I don't. Thank God. We live in this weird strip of suburb where you can choose either East High or Pound High. My sisters and brothers chose East High. So I chose Pound. I did this as a purely self-protective measure. My sisters, especially Lizzie, would have pursued, tortured, and harassed me endlessly if I set foot or even thought about setting foot near them. No, sir. High school would've become my own personal Spanish Inquisition crossed with Salem Witch Trials crossed with every movie you've ever seen with a marine sergeant torturing his underlings at boot camp. No thanks, folks. No way.

I cannot give Lizzie that pleasure.

Now, this brings us to my mom. Who is essentially the only decent one in the house. But if you think post-Chocula she went out and found the perfect husband, you can guess again. The guy she got is six foot three, three hundred pounds, and stands in front of us at the buffet line my mom sets out at dinner, eating all the food. If we are lucky we will get something good but you better grab it while you still have a chance. He never talks to us, except in grunts, and then goes straight to his room after dinner, to lie on his water bed and watch *Wheel of Fortune*.

So, basically, my real dad is a vampire and my stepdad is an ogre. If my mom gets married a third time it will clearly be to either a werewolf or a mummy. I'm sure she married this guy so her kids would have a home and all but, man oh man, I wish she could have found someone that made her happy.

I have an escape plan for Mom and me where we can leave all these jerkfaces in the dust, but I am only on stage 2 of that plan currently.

I'm looking at her in the kitchen and realizing that if you made a trajectory from Brigitte Bardot to Mrs. Santa Claus, my mom is one-third of the way from Brigitte Bardot over. She's a total dumpling about everything and certainly deserves better than this crap-hole.

"Honey, did anything exciting happen at your first day of school today?"

"Not really. Logan McDonough got a moped."

She's making Mexican casserole, which is heavy on the rotation and usually lands on a Monday night, unless there's gonna be Taco Tuesday.

"Oh, I bet that was a real hit."

"Not really. Becky told him he was a nerd on wheels."

"Well, that wasn't very nice of her."

"*Tsh*. Whatever. She's kind of a bitch."

"Honey, you know I don't like words like that."

"I know. She's just not very nice is all."

"Well, did you say something nice to him? I bet that woulda made his day."

"What?! No. Becky would kill me."

Now Mom stops putting the chips in the casserole and looks up. Real emphasis.

"You know what, honey, just because Becky does something doesn't mean you have to do it."

"Yeah, right. She's like the number one most popular girl, Mom."

"Well, why is that?"

"I dunno, she was like a model or something."

"A model?"

"Yeah."

"A model for what, might I ask, seeing as we live in this bastion of the fashion industry here in Lincoln, Nebraska?"

"I dunno. I think, like, the J. C. Penney catalog?"

"Oh, well that explains it."

"Mom, you just don't understand, okay?"

"Honey, all I'm saying is that you can stand up to her—"

"You mean like you do with Dad?"

But she doesn't take the bait. She just ignores me and puts the casserole in the oven instead. Doesn't matter, my brothers run in from the back and start tearing through the cupboards like the Four Horsemen of the Apocalypse are riding up from Kansas.

"Boys, now listen, it's only one hour to dinner. I don't want you to ruin your appetites."